Charles Mackinnon

Essays on the Following Subjects

wealth and force of nations, authenticity of Ossian, accompanyment, existence of

body, fortification, battle

Charles Mackinnon

Essays on the Following Subjects
wealth and force of nations, authenticity of Ossian, accompanyment, existence of body, fortification, battle

ISBN/EAN: 9783337267919

Printed in Europe, USA, Canada, Australia, Japan

Cover: Foto ©Andreas Hilbeck / pixelio.de

More available books at **www.hansebooks.com**

E S S A Y S

ON THE

FOLLOWING SUBJECTS:

WEALTH AND FORCE OF NATIONS,

AUTHENTICITY OF OSSIAN,

ACCOMPANYMENT,

EXISTENCE OF BODY,

FORTIFICATION,

BATTLE.

O

By CHARLES M'KINNON, Efq;

EDINBURGH.
Printed for WILLIAM CREECH.
M,DCC,LXXXV,

ERRATA.

Note to pag. 25. line 10.

Even confidering money as fixed capital, it can caufe production as the addition of any other fort can; and, befides, can caufe the production of any fort of fixed capital or commodity that is wanted.

Pag. 78. Before the words " The opinions anfwer-" ed above" there ought to have been a break * * * * for the expreffion refers to the 7 Sections.

OBSERVATIONS*

ON THE

WEALTH AND FORCE

OF

NATIONS.

* This was firſt printed in 1781.

TO THE

MEMORY

OF

DAVID HUME.

" *Say, ſhall my little bark attendant ſail?*"

OBSERVATIONS, &c.

Of Nations supposed to have no dealings with others.

THE expence, annual (for instance) of a nation, is supplied from its income during that period, and the savings of former years. Whatever a man believe to be the first, a few lines will hold his account of the second.

Progress

IF a man propoſes to make a piece of clothing, an ornament, or a weapon, he muſt lay in food to ſubſiſt himſelf while he is about it. If he employs another man to furniſh him any ſuch things, he muſt give him food, if he has it not of his own. What was once a luxury, is, in proceſs of time, held a conveniency, and may afterwards be held a neceſſary. Now, it is the ſame thing whether a man gives another articles, or the food to ſubſiſt thoſe who make them.

Income Annual (for inſtance) *of Nations.*

THE firſt attempt to aſcertain this, worth mentioning, was made ſome little time ago

by

by Quefnai, firft phyfician to the King of
France. It has been fupported by many
refpectable men. His opinion was, the
income of a country was its commodities,
with this limitation, that artifans added nothing to the national income. They did
not produce the materials they worked on.
The fociety, therefore, received by their labour only one fort of commodities inftead
of another neceffarily confumed in fabricating it.

The next is that of Doctor Smith, imagined, I believe, without any affiftance
from the œconomifts, though not publifhed till very lately. It is, ' That the
' annual revenue of every fociety is always
' precifely equal to the exchangeable value
' of the whole annual produce of its indu-
' ftry ; or rather, is precifely the fame thing
' with that exchangeable value.' For *rich*
is the word by which we exprefs that a
perfon or a nation has many commodities ;
and whatever opinion may be entertained

of

of human capacity and steadiness, few fabricate what is not of some use to themselves or others.

A man bestows any income on any number of people: It will not be disputed that the income he gives may be the same, whether they live in his house or not; whether they fabricate any thing for him or not: That he may get the same work done by them, whether they live in his house or not. Supposing, now, on the one side, that they are absolutely idle, and, on the other, that they do more or less work for him : In this last case, he has, from any income, the same benefit as if, in the former, he had the same income, with as much more as would procure the work. Supposing a man gets any quantity of work done, and another gets the same work done for less income, this last is, for the time, in respect to the former, in the same situation as if he had as much more income as

the

the difference of income beftowed amounts to.

Suppofing the income the fame, and that work can be got for the fame price, it will be held a matter of indifference whether the work is executed or not.

But who are the employers? What I have faid in the former Sect. leads me to think that all others are employed by the holders of the food.

If it is obferved, that the more government takes from any clafs of people, the lefs it has for itfelf, and the lefs it can give others, it is of little confequence to a country whether the government ftates its income to be the food; or the food, with fome articles held the moft neceffary; the whole produce of the land with the œconomifts, or even with Smith, the produce of 'all the 'lands and all the labour.'

B   *Hoards.*

Hoards.

FOOD, clothing, lodging, amufement, fhow, war, medicine, and travelling, with the inftruments ufed in providing them, are all the commodities of any country. In the following obfervations, I confider the national income, the condition of the people, and the revenue of government, in nations where the labourers are free, and bufinefs carried on by perfons who advance their capitals. The reafonings do not depend, on my opinion, upon the income of nations: I explained it at fo great length, chiefly becaufe it fhowed a method to ftudy the fcience.

Variations

THE quantity of commodities in any country is greater or lefs, as the people are able and willing to produce. Their ability and inclination may be fuch, that the wealth may go on increafing, till it reaches its greateft poffible height; may continue long the fame; may diminifh for a long time; or a flux and reflux may take place; on the balance of which, in any period, it is found to have increafed, to be the fame, or to have diminifhed.

Few, if any, are equally fit for bufinefs the whole time they continue in it. Some may know more, attend more than thofe whofe places they fill, and increafe their capital; others may be only equal to their prede-

predeceffors, and keep their capitals the fame; others again, may know lefs, attend lefs, than thofe who went before them, and are not able to keep up the capitals they received. Differences in the qualities of the labourers may alfo have an effect.

No art, once made public, is loft, the danger, expence, &c. of which the employers are willing to reward, and the employed to rifk; difcoveries are continually made; the capacity of men, as well as their knowledge, increafes; and, when men err in chufing their projects, they ufually err on the fafe fide.

The increafe in the production may begin from the holder of the food (for example) wifhing to fecure his fubfiftence, or get fome particular article; or he who otherwife would not have exerted himfelf,

is

is tempted by the articles the artifan lays before him.

The narrower the competition in the fale of any commodity is, it may be expected that thofe who produce it are capable of lefs exertion ; that they will exact lefs work from the labourers they employ, and be more indifferent about the quantity of it : The labourers, therefore, are lefs fkilful, dexterous, and lefs able to bear fatigue.

Men may voluntarily produce lefs,

For fear of not getting fale.

Finding, or prefuming, that a quantity of goods, fold at a higher price, gives as much or more profit, than a greater quantity fold at a lower rate.

The

The uncertainty how much of the fruits of their labour they will be deprived of, the hopes of having warning for one, five, twenty years; the fear of quarrels : Thefe may affect their induftry for ages.

Of the *Labour of Soldiers, Menial Servants,* &c.

IF, inftead of ten perfons (for inftance) twelve of equal fkill, dexterity, and induftry, are employed in producing commodities, there muft be more produced; that is, in the view I place things, the difference, as far as employed in fome occupations, augments the income ; employed in others, the income does more.

The income that fupports perfons of fuch occupations, will fuppoit artifans.

The

The increase in the production, will not follow immediately upon the increase in the number of hands employed in productive occupations.

It may happen, that there follows no diminution of commodities from even a considerable diminution of hands.

The national income may be the same, whether the portion of it laid out on persons of such occupations, be bestowed on troops or footmen.

Cheapness.

MANY who would not give twelve days labour for an article, would be tempted to exert themselves, if it cost but six.

Enterprise.

Enterprife. .

OUR daily obfervation, and the accounts we have of the different countries, defective as they are, entitle us to conjecture,

That a nation may advance more quickly than fome who muft make exertions abfolutely greater; and that it may keep an even pace with others.

That a nation may go on equally with fome whofe fituation is eafier than its own, or may get before others. ,

That nations whofe fituation is equal, may advance equally, or that fome may get before others.

Where

Where the government is not mixed, and the competition is open, we may expect to find almost the whole of a nation of the one character, as far as the communication is open.

As European nations now are, I think increasing the difficulties would retard.

Hoards.

COMMODITIES are employed,

As capital.

As income in producing commodities.

As income in rewarding unproductive labour.

C   People

People confume the clothes (for inftance) they have; government its arms, &c.

It is well known to what a degree the droughts in rice countries, infects in others, drift ice in Iceland, &c. render the reproduction of food precarious.

Government may put together its hoards of military ftores in one year, (for inftance) or gradually in ten. So it may any hoards of food it makes for armies, &c.

Of the Extent of Capital required to carry on National Bufinefs.

Suppose two countries, of which the produce (for example) of the land, in the year (for inftance) is equal; that, in the one, the whole is in one crop; in the other, in two equal crops; and that, in it, the

the payment for the firft crop comes in foon enough to carry on the cultivation of the fecond. In the former, it is vifible that twice the capital is required to produce the fame total.

I have not endeavoured to calculate how fmall a capital may employ the artifans of any country.

Suppofe two countries, of which the fales are equal; that, in the one, the accounts are paid in fix months; in the other, in twelve: In this laft the merchants muft have twice the capital.

Divifion of Capital.

WHETHER the capital be divided among ten, or among forty men, fo much of their profits as are not added to their capital, will equally give income to the people.

The

The former are more tempted to rival any fuperior orders that may be in the ftate.

The competition among the latter is ftronger than among the former. From particular accidents, indeed, the competition among the ten may be fometimes as ftrong, or ftronger, than among the forty; but we cannot expect this to happen often, or to continue long.

Of Fixed Capital.

In inclofing a field (for inftance) with a wall of ftone and lime, more capital is diffipated at firft than if it is inclofed with dry ftone, and more capital is diffipated afterwards; in keeping up the laft.

Shipping are a fixed capital, that coft much in building, in keeping them up

while

while they are worth repairing; and they are fometimes totally loft.

Diminution of Money Capital.

IT may be of great confequence, what proportion in production is effected by fixed capital.

In Britain (for example) the farmer (for inftance) can raife but one crop of corn in the year.

Suppofe that there are fome years to run of the leafe of a farmer (for inftance) the fall in the price may leffen his capital confiderably, before he gets fuch a deduction in his rent as the change of affairs requires.

Money.

Money.

DAVID HUME, with the perfpicuity natural to his vaft mind, has fhowed, how an addition to the quantity of money increafes the production of a country; and the bad effects of a diminution in the money. And Dr Smith has reprefented it as a kind of fixed capital.

I propofe to begin the comparifon of the effects caufed by bringing more figns to fale, with thofe caufed by bringing more confumable commodities; of the effects caufed by a diminution of figns, with thofe caufed by a diminution of confumable commodities.

All thefe may affect the fixed capital of the nation.

Few

Few chufe to let capital lie long idle.

Where the income is at its greateft pof-fible height, the commodity introduced, if fold, can only hinder the fale, or lower the price of others in competition with it: The effect muft be the fame, if it caufes no production.

The addition of confumable commodities caufes production,

By keeping labourers more employed.

By increafing the labouring hands.

Caufing exertion among undertakers, by lowering the price of commodities.

The production caufed vifibly may be various; except from rafh project, it can-not be more than the production fells for.

'The

the addition may caufe no production,

If it increafe not the number of labouring hands,

If it employs them not more fully.

When fold to undertakers, it does not tempt a certain exertion. Though it caufes none one year (for inftance) if continued, it may.

The effect is the fame, if it caufes no production.

When the income is at its greateft pofſible height, the addition of figns can only lower the value of the figns already in circulation.

The addition of figns caufes production,

By

By the price of labour not rifing immediately in proportion to the addition.

The addition caufes no production,

From falling into the hands of people
unwilling or unable to effect it.

The production can go on, while an addition of figns procures more labour; which
will be, till the proportion of figns and
commodities is the fame, as among the o-
ther figns and commodities in the country.

The proportion, therefore, of the fign
to the greateft production caufed by it, is
the fame as that of the money circulating
in a country, to the money price of all the
commodities fold in it: This may be various; but the quantity of money in every
country is far lefs than the money price of
the goods fold.

D   A

A diminution of commodities caufes a
diminution of the production,

By leffening the labouring hands.

When, in confequence of the diminution, hands are lefs employed.

Relaxing exertion, by heightening the
price of the commodities that would have
been in competition with them.

The diminution caufed may be various;
except from caution, it cannot exceed its
price in the commodities diminifhed.

The diminution does not leffen the production,

If it does not leffen the labouring hands,

If there is ftill enough left to employ the
labourers as they would have been,

When

When it does not relax exertion.

The effect of the diminution of confumable commodities here, is to heighten the price, or caufe the fale, of the commodities with which they would have been in competition.

The diminution of figns leffens the production,

By the price of labour not falling fo much, as that the figns remaining will employ all who were employed before. In this fituation nothing can keep up the price of labour, but the labourers being forced to pay a certain price for the commodities they purchafe: That price may be fuch as to caufe a diminution in the number of labouring hands, greater or lefs.

The diminution of figns does not leffen the production,

If there is ftill enough left to keep all the hands employed as they would have been.

The diminution caufed may be various; it cannot exceed the production that would have been caufed by the addition of the figns gone, to the remainder in the country.

It is obvious, that the progrefs of increafe and diminution, however caufed, may be regular and uninterrupted, or not; more or lefs rapid; and may take more or lefs time.

Money, whether metal, falt, or fhells, is of fo much furer fale, that other commodities rarely perform the office of figns: I have not known one inftance of it.

The increafe of figns or commodities renders it eafier to increafe capital; the diminution renders it more difficult to keep
capital

capital entire, and may render it impoffible.

Poverty.

A part of the national income is de-
ftroyed, or its fource ftopped up; fome
propofe to produce a lefs quantity of any
commodity; cultivators, artifans, &c. choofe
to employ fewer hands; in confequence,
more or lefs labouring people may be obliged to try new trades, in competition with
thofe eftablifhed in them, on whom they
may encroach more or lefs. The mifery
or deaths which follow, have not, I believe,
been afcertained in any one cafe: There
may be more or lefs. Though none may
die, literally of hunger, yet no fmall number of grown perfons, and many children,
may die of difeafes brought on by fcanty
or unwholefome nourifhment, bad lodging,

or

or clothing; befides, that difeafes owing to none of them, lie heavier on perfons in fuch circumftances.

Slaves may fuffer lefs from this than free labourers.

Population.

IT appears that neither the marriages, births, nor deaths, bear a fixed proportion to the numbers of men, nor near it: Nor do the fexes bear an uniform proportion to one another.

A nation may have the fame income with another more or lefs numerous.

Much of the labour done in one country by cattle or machines, may be done in another by human animals.

Suppofe

Suppofe any income divided among any number of people,

The income may increafe, and their numbers remain the fame.

The population may increafe, while the income refts the fame.

Either may diminifh, while the other remains as it was.

The people may increafe fafter than the income, and the income may increafe fafter than the people.

The people may diminifh fafter than the income, and the income may diminifh fafter than the people.

Both may increafe or diminifh equally: Both may ftand ftill.

In all the countries we know, almoft every man would, from one motive or o-

ther,

ther, marry *, if he thought he could have what is, in the idea of the times and country, a fubfiftence for his family.

Surely the income may diminifh fo far, as that fewer can rear families.

Where the income has been for fome. time the fame, it is probable moft of the people have fmall portions; perhaps ftill more generally in fuch as are far advanced in the arts: in thefe, the women may earn more, and the children earn earlier.

Of the Revenue of the Government.

GOVERNMENT may take any article from thofe who have produced it, or from thofe who have got it of them.

Whatever

* Confider the cafe of the Lazeroni at Naples.

Whatever part of the income of any clafs of people government takes, the clafs has the lefs fcr itfelf, and the others can get the lefs from it.

Government may either give away the whole again among the people, or hoard a part. However great the portion govern- ment takes may be, the income of the na- tion may ftill remain the fame : Though it may buy dear, or fell cheap ; yet thofe in- to whofe hands it gets through government, may be as able and willing to take care of themfelves as other people ; but, as it may not beftow its income on thofe it came from, individuals may fuffer greatly.

Many are furprifed, that a man of any moderate underftanding fhould not obferve, that income would circulate through the nation from the hands of the fubjects, as well as from thofe of the prince ; and that the outlays of the prince would circulate as well, if beftowed on canals and high-

E   ways;

ways, troops and military ſtores, as on pa-
laces, gardens, and agreeable attendants.
Such has been the progreſs of man in every inquiry of faĉt and exiſtence.

As ſoon as additional rent can be afforded, government, in ſome caſes, no doubt,
ought to take it ; in others, it ought to abſtain for a longer or ſhorter time.

Where the ſubjeĉts know not how much
of the produce of the land (for example)
government ſhall exaĉt, ſome may enterpriſe in hopes of defrauding the government, and are diſappointed ; the national
income of the year (for inſtance) may not
be leſſened by their enterpriſe ; their capital may ; the diſpute may coſt government
ſomething ; and the example may leſſen
the ſcandal attending injuſtice and fraud,
where government is concerned.

An exciſe on a commodity may be a tax
on the rent, on the tenant, on the produ-
cer,

eer, on the labourers employed in producing it, or on the confumer, as accident determines. Labouring perfons are the leaft able to hold out in combination, from their poverty and their numbers.

It may happen, that the falary paid to working people, though perhaps not the price of labour, is by fuch taxes raifed fo, the national income not increafing faft enough, that for feveral there is but a fcanty fubfiftence, and for fome none.

Laying an excife on a luxury may caufe lefs of it to be produced ; but, it has been obferved, that moft men are not induced to quit their country but by very great difficulties. Such a tax may retard the advances of a country, by raifing the price of the article; for what does not allure one, may allure another.

Even in countries which have not reached their greateft poffible height, if, inftead
of

of laying on the whole in land taxes a large
fum were laid on luxuries, I believe that
the fmall proprietors would almoft always,
in the courfe of a life, have more to themfelves, after paying what they chofe of the
excifes.

The greater portion each perfon has of
the national income, the more government
can take from him. A tax on the neceffaries of life will hinder people from breed-
ing, if high enough.

Suppofe a nation has an annual income,
which we fhall phrafe twenty millions.
Suppofe another nation of only half its
numbers; but which, by fuperior art or
induftry, has the fame income. Suppofe
in both the income at its greateft poffible
height, keeping war and peftilence out of
the queftion.

Perhaps, by laying a poll-tax in fmalls,
by the week (for inftance) a confiderable
fum

ſum might be got, without much oppreſ-
ſion, of the moſt thoughtleſs; at worſt,
government might make uſe of it, to get
at the income of thoſe who would not
conſume the commodities it choſe to tax.

Of Bounties, Regulations, &c.

IT may happen, that the induſtry of
ſome part of the people is employed in objects leſs beneficial to themſelves and the
ſtate.

In any art, uſeful methods may be
known in one province that are not known
in others; they may be borrowed from
foreign nations; diſcoveries may be made:
Theſe, however valuable, may be adopted
but ſlowly. I do not know whether men
will ever be able to prove that the ſkill of
any country is ſuch, that more cannot be
done.

Some

Some men, had they capital, might ac-
complish defigns, which would, in more
or lefs time, replace to government an out-
lay.

The intereft of no one clafs of people is
neceffarily the fame with that of the ftate.
The produce of a piece of ground may be
as 20, leaving a profit of 10; or it may be
as 16, leaving a profit of 9: The bufinefs
of fifhing may, in fome degree, admit fimilar variations; the artifan may have
profit in his bufinefs, 10 or 15, as he ma-
nages it; production may be effected by
machines and cattle, or by labourers paying taxes; while the national income has
advanced (for inftance) a feventh, the population has advanced a fifth, and the employment of the labourers lefs fecure.

A queftion will, on thefe views, occur,
what government may gain by beftowing
money, or by penal regulations?

The

The more fimple the inquiry, the more honefty and fimplicity are in the character of the fubjects, the lefs any change propofed croffes their ideas of their own intereft, or their vanity ; the lefs the government is difturbed by parties, the lefs vigour is required in adminiftration.

The outlay may be raifed from fo many, that each fhall not regard what he pays to it.

Giving the aid in one fum may often be very proper; government may give only what it pleafes ; but perfons of the beft intentions may fail often in their projects ; government may be impofed on, and many may enter more haftily into bad fchemes, or indulge themfelves in pernicious expences, from hopes of having a confiderable part, if not the whole, of their outlay replaced by government.

On

On these accounts, it may often be thought proper to give the affiftance according to the quantity produced, however great that be. Hurt may follow from discontinuing the affiftance given in this manner. The weaknefs or corruption in the government may increafe fo far, that this, too, may be given to fuch as have not laboured for it.

Government is ftill more expofed to miftake, in endeavouring to difcover what chance it has of changing the direction of national induftry, and how much it ought to lay out on fuch views: It can more eafily difcover whether the change propofed is beneficial, at leaft to fuch a degree as to make it proper in it to venture.

Premiums are given merely for difcoveries in the arts; the expence of them is fuppofed to be a matter of indifference to the ftate.

Such,

Such, however, has hitherto been the frame of man, that, if a rule were to be laid down over the whole world, for ages, there is no room to hesitate a moment in deciding, that government ought to interfere no farther than to give its subjects security in their property; all the confidence possible, that they shall enjoy the fruits of their labour; prevent all restraints on competition in the production; make these works that private persons would not, or could not do, as roads, canals; and reward discoveries in the arts.

The more profit any person makes in his business, the more government may get from him; on the other hand, the wider the competition, the more each man strives to produce as much as he can, as good as he can, and as cheap as he can. Cheapness may, besides giving the government, by different ways, opportunity to increase its revenue, make the revenue more valuable.

F   About

About a century ago, pecuniary encou‑
ragements were offered in France to mar‑
riages contracted fo early as twenty years.
A man who had a wife and the profpect of
a family, may be expected to exert himfelf
more: When the young ones born in con‑
fequence are grown up, the fall of labour,
from the greater number of labourers, and
the invention of thefe more quickened, en‑
ables the undertaker to execute more pro‑
ject with the fame capital. If many mar‑
riages followed in confequence, there muft
not only more children of the poor die,
but a greater proportion of them, if the
increafe of exertion of the parents, and the
aid of government, did not prevent it. The
aid here was an exemption from a pernici‑
ous tax; a fmall fum, not a reafonable en‑
couragement to marriage.

Where the aid is given to fuch as would
marry without it, as well as to thofe who
would not, which was done here, there is
no reafon to expect that the benefit will
compenfate

compenfate fuch an out-lay. To difcover all, or nearly all, who would not marry without the aid, is perhaps the inquiry, of all others, in which government has the leaft reafon to expect fuccefs. As France then was, it is probable that even the vigorous adminiftration of Colbert was no way equal to the tafk *.

A cafe may be fuppofed, in which people ought to be had, in cafe of wars or contagious diftempers. I know no country in which it has been proper to lay out any thing on that account.

Of foreign Trade.

I STATE, on one fide, the clafs of artifans, and, on the other, thofe who fupply

every

* I have fometimes fufpected that this edict was only a ftroke of court addrefs.

every article of expence that itſelf does not make.

It is more advantageous for government to have both ſides of the exchange in the country than only one. It can chuſe where to lay its taxes; whence to levy its troops; even the command of the greater number of people for this laſt uſe, may ſometimes be of the utmoſt conſequence.

Caſe Firſt.

THE exchange of commodities produced by either claſs in one nation, for thoſe of the ſame claſs in another.

Cafe Second.

EXCHANGE of the artifan commodities of one nation for thofe of the other clafs of a fecond.

The demand for the commodities of one may be more fteady than for thofe of the other.

The commodities of the one clafs may be of more ufe at home, upon a ftagnation, than thofe of the other.

On a rupture, the effect of the greater command of neceffaries may be great: Government can always find people able to make arms.

Either

Either may come to have both fides of the exchange, within itfelf, fooner than the other.

It is better in the monarchies of Europe, and even in the greater republics, to tax rent, than profit of capitals.

Artifans within a country have fuch ad-ntages which foreigners have not, that ney cannot fail to draw to themfelves, in the end, any bufinefs they aim at, if the country produces the materials they work on. In the great nations of Europe, the national income is increafing ; tafte changes continually ; novelty pleafes. Some com-modities, and the materials of fome manu-factures, are confined to certain countries by climate ; the weight of correfpondence, ftock, and fkill, is great ; fo that foreign-ers ftill fell much to all of them, and would fell more, if they were not reftrained.

Cafe

Cafe Third.

THE above, with what I have faid on mines of money metals, in my remarks on the home trade, fhow all I have to fay on the money balance.

Reftraints on Importation.

PEOPLE who muft ftruggle through a great competition to make money, will be lefs apt to throw it away than thofe who fee they have few rivals.

Bounties

THE bounty may lower the money price of a commodity.

More of it being produced, the exportation, and the apprehenfion of it, having lefs effect than the greatnefs of the quantity brought to market. I have heard no proof of a fingle inftance of this, though it muft have happened.

The increafe in the production may be caufed,

By drawing capital from other employments. When intereft is given for loans, (*i. e.* almoft always) nobody keeps his money in his defk.

Employing

Employing as capital, circulating or fixed, what would have been employed as income.

By exerting more fkill or induftry.

It has always been propofed to give this
bounty on the produ&ion, no matter how
produced ; it therefore tends to improve
methods, no more than many other equal
fpurs to induftry.

If the produ&ion is caufed merely by
force of capital, and the price of the commodity is lowered, the capital may, fooner or later, be leffened ; and continually
leffened, till it be diffipated.

Will the produ&ion caufed by the money balance gained by the bounty, often
make up to government the revenue it
cofts ?

G   Many

Many will exert themfelves for the forced, that would not for the natural price. Others will be confirmed in their inactivity and bad methods, by the greater probability of fale.

People go moft readily into the employments that are neareft their own, as the farmer into the gardening, the weaver in wool into weaving flax.

Regulations on importation and exportation may hinder variations in the price of a commodity : Bounties on both hinder lefs ones : To difcover when the advantages of fuch bounties compenfate the expence, and what expence, requires nice information indeed. It may fafely be affirmed, that not a man in Britain has ever poffeffed it in any one cafe.

Comparifon

LESS time is required to bring in the returns in many branches of the foreign trade, than in many of the domeſtic ; but more time is needed generally to bring in the returns when the ſale is made abroad, than if it had been made at home.

It is better for a nation to have the ſame amount of employment, by people within the country, than by foreigners, as the employ is expoſed to fewer cauſes of failure.

Obſerva-

Obſervations on the Force of Shepherd Na-
tions againſt the ſtanding Armies of Na-
tions farther advanced in Society.

I.

WE may expect leſs patience in ſhepherds than in the others, and alſo leſs a-
cuteneſs in their deſigns.

II.

Methods of fighting abandoned on the
beſt grounds, may have great ſucceſs for
ſome time, becauſe the manner of oppoſing them is forgot; but, when one of
theſe has had ſucceſs much taken notice of,
an effectual way of oppoſing it, is ſooner
or later found out; in proceſs of time it
is diſcovered that the method of fighting
muſt

muſt be varied more or leſs, when the methods made uſe of by the enemy are different.

It is probable that barbarians will be
found leſs liable to panic, except thoſe ri-
ſing from ſuperſtition, than civilized troops;
particularly from being oppoſed by methods unknown to them. In courſe of
time it is found, that exerciſe before the
war, and patience in the beginning, will
prevent the panic.

Attempts openly made will ſucceed often, even with ſhepherds, from the very
idea of the boldneſs neceſſary to make
them. It is diſcovered that troops whoſe
minds and limbs have been occupied on
theſe, will eaſily diſappoint them.

A ſtanding army, which never has ſeen
the face of an enemy, may often do great
things, merely becauſe they do not know
but that they are done every day.

It

It is allowed, that fortreſſes are of no uſe but to hold magazines, command roads, rivers, canals, or make it eaſier for armies to command them ; the expence beſtowed on feeding them muſt be great indeed, and improper, except from the view of foreign aid, if they can hold out long, after the country is ruined.

III.

Hunting nations, when they can be truſted, are by far the beſt ſcouts. A civilized nation might make great uſe of ſhepherds, particularly riding nations, to lay waſte an enemy's country. If the Ruſſian court apprehended the loſs of much power or territory, it would, without ſcruple, let looſe their Coſſacks, &c. What devaſtation could the peaſants of Germany do, in compariſon to theſe, under the direction of Ruſſian officers ?

IV.

IV.

War, as other arts, is continually improving ; the capacity of men is fo too. Yet, from the good fenfe, humanity. love .of quiet, averfion to fatigue, felfifhnefs, fear of encountering dangers which are new, the want of epidemical paffions, and of blind prejudice in favour of one's felf in its people, a nation, in the laft ftages of fociety, may be conquered, province by province, or perhaps even at once, by any fhepherd nation that chufes to attack it. No art, by which a reward of wealth, rank, or fame, proportioned to its difficulty, &c. is not gained, will be followed by many. There feems to have been a progrefs of fraud in the management of the pecuniary interefts of government.

Among people fo warlike and active as the Europeans, chivalry muft have retarded the progrefs of civilization ; it added to
the

the caufes of war *, and of diverting from luxury people little addicted to literary a-mufements of any kind.

A particular Cafe.

It has been faid, that the Pruffian empire is upon diet ; that the Britifh empire is in that ftate in which the phyfician allows his patient to do what he pleafes, will be held by many of thofe who confider all the circumftances of its condition.

There is no harm in my printing an inquiry, whether a fcheme be not the beft that a bad fituation allows. It is, to drop the fleet. We are at war with a combination far fuperior to us in power. Though, by the whim of human affairs we fhould

get

---

* The hurt of private war is well known.

get out of this, with little or no lofs of
territory, we muft expect to be foon in
war again. War adds little to our taxes ;
our country is not the feat of it ; we are
republicans, cut off, in fome meafure, from
the world ; no wonder if we are readier to
enter into war than any other people. The
wars we have begun, merely to get a choice
of markets to fell goods, are well known.
The expence laid out by the French and
Spaniards on their fleets, fhows they are
refolved to defend their colonies, and makes
it probable they will perfift for fome time
in fchemes depending on naval force. Have
we any title or reafon to expect that they
will leave us any thing they think themfelves at liberty to take ?

The grandeur of the French monarchy
feemed to difpenfe it from the precautions
neceffary to other powers : But may not a
minifter arife, who will facrifice connection enough to give the monarchy the ef-

H   fect

fect that its wealth, and the character of
its subjects entitle it to ?

It is more difficult to form troops in Britain than on the Continent ; and the dif-
pofition of Parliament, the army appearing
lefs neceffary to us, led miniftry to make
ufe of military command as rank and pen-
fion *.   When the army was more neceffary, ours might be little inferior to thofe
of our neighbours : The country could now
maintain a great one.

It is probable that few capitals would
quit the country.   In fome countries, the
rank of a merchant is lefs honourable, as is
that of a fubject who has no power at
court ; many would think a fubject of the
Britifh government a higher condition than
the fubject of a fimple monarchy ; in o-
                                              thers

* In the late trials of the two Admirals, the fleet,
after every allowance to be made for party, and for newf-
paper manoeuvres, made an appearance that was little
expected.

thers the profits are lefs, and they would
have to contend with abilities more fhar-
pened than their own ; in others no more
fale than at home ; in all they would be
ftrangers, and in fome find their country-
men their competitors ; ftock could no
where be fo eafily managed as at home.
Some capitals would perhaps be taken or
forced out of the fhipping bufinefs with
lofs *.

Reftraining Ireland made the employ
more certain : The Irifh could buy more
foon after the reftraints were taken off :
Few have full grounds to guefs whether
they would buy more from us or not, except court dreffes, which the fovereignty
of the King would fecure. How far the
influ-

---

* On the different employments of capital, on foreign
trade, and money, I refer to what has been faid by
Hume, Smith, and above. As to the reft, thofe who
entered into fuch trade as we were in, would one way
or other make room for us.

influence and example of the court would extend the confumption of Britifh drefles among the middling claffes of people, not many have a title to conjecture.

The exportation of fhips, iron, &c. from America, would probably not be reftrained.

The other commodities we get from the Colonies and the Eaft Indies are fuch, that, even in this country, the influence and example of the court would limit the ufe of them to very narrow bounds, without any regulation. If fuch as our country did not produce were entirely prohibited, a very moderate exertion would hinder any importation worth noticing. The muflins, fugar, &c. fold us by foreigners, would furely be as proper a fubject of taxation as the fugar, &c. fold us by ourfelves. If drawbacks were then given, it would be for reafons on which no ftrefs is laid at prefent. We fhould then have a wider market

market to buy moft of thefe commodities in, and in no cafe a narrower.

From the ruins of the Mogul empire powerful ftates have rifen ; war is improving in the country, which, befides, has been long polifhed. It cannot be expected that the diftance of India fhould not affect deeply the condition of the people, and the management of the revenue after it comes in. The bulk of the Whites, and fome natives who were in favour, or expected it, might, perhaps, for a long time, prefer the diftant government; it is more certain, that almoft the whole of the natives would prefer an independent one in the country, even a White and a Chriftian one.

Accordingly, the military force fent over, has always been fmall, and fent by ftealth.

Leaving the territories in the hands of the Company, government might draw
fome

some money from it, and reward some servants, by giving them or their friends places in the country; taking them into its own hands, it could reward many more, and draw more money, or the same money with less oppression, as its management would probably be more vigorous than that of the Company; threatening to take them is a middle way. When government had ..ore to give, its servants would crave more. How much would the high price be lowered, when the fund which afforded it was greatly lessened, or lost?

Without any dissertation upon the quadrille party on the Continent, it will be allowed, that there is no occasion for our interference to stop any preponderating power: When there shall, the more rest we have, the more we can do.

The longer it is deferred, the more our burthens are increased.

The

The increase of the national debt may lead the people to wish for monarchy, as the only chance they have of getting rid of it.

Confined to Britain and Ireland, the situation of the King would be more enviable than that of any monarch in Europe.

If undertaken, it would be easily executed.

Why not undertaken, and that immediately ?

* * * * *

Hic multa desiderantur.

When I read the within, I am tempted to think, that I too am a painter; but,
when

when I confider that expectation has been analyfed, I relapfe into my natural fcepti-cifm, and reft fatisfied, that,

De las cofas mas feguras
La mas fegura es dudar.

O F T H E

AUTHENTICITY

O F

O S S I A N.

I

AUTHENTICITY of OSSIAN.

I PROPOSE only a few thoughts on this subject, without pretending to decide the question. They are the ideas of one who never saw any of the supposed Gaelic copy but what M'Pherson has printed, and the Episode which introduces the Fourth Book of Fingal, with two not inconsiderable variations, addressed to a person very different from Malvina.

I.

THE ideas are those of a great poet.

This

This has been denied, becaufe of different circumftances.

A mode of expreffion which is not ufed either in Englifh, French, Italian, or Spanifh, ' *the tree of the ruftling leaf;*' ' *the fields of my reft;*' ' *the bed of thy repofe;*' this is much ufed in the Gaelic.

There is no language but has modes of expreffion which appear to a certain eye, or to all eyes, on fome occafions, ridiculous, if the words of another language are thrown into them. Tranflate word for word into Englifh the phrafes, ' *qu'il fuffit d'un fana-* ' *tique pour;*' ' Le propre du fanatifme eft ' *d'echauffer les têtes;*' ' Quelques perfon- ' nes proferent *des paroles* indifcretes et vi- ' olentes;' yet thefe expreffions are conftantly ufed by the moft claffical French authors. We know but little of the Latin language; yet, it cannot be denied, that many paffages of the Epiftolae Obfcurorum Virorum, and Swift's Latinitas Grattania-

na

na are ridiculous, merely becaufe we know the mode of expreffion is that of a modern language, and are fure it is very different from the Roman.

In the Gaelic, the expreffion ' field of my ' reft,' or ' my field of reft,' is (for inftance) preferable to that ' field where I reft,' as it expreffes the fame idea in fewer founds and in fewer words.

II.

In tracing the different fteps by which language arrived to what it now is, Smith found an employment not beneath his genius; many refpectable men had failed in it; much lefs genius is required to gain one or more of the fteps: In polifhed times people are pretty much tied down to what was made in times lefs refined. Accordingly, one cannot examine a page of the beft books in Englifh, French, or Italian authors,

thors, if he does it in this view, without feeing that the language is fcarce any where what one would wifh it, in any refpect. Each has faults in idiom, figure, and conftruction peculiar to itfelf; and the idiom, figure, and conftruction of all are confined by cuftom within too narrow limits. In all of them, too, one is forced to ufe many more founds and words, on almoft every occafion, than he would wifh if he ftudies the matter ever fo little. The Latin is, in this refpect, far fuperior to any of the languages above mentioned; yet, even in writing hiftory, Tacitus found it fluggifh. This fault muft be ftill more felt when one fpeaks in public than in hiftory, and yet ftill more in poetry. In poetry, it will be more felt in figured than in plain ftyle, as that may very eafily be too long; in general, where the mind is moft to be moved, the paffage would gain moft by being in few words and founds.

It

It is fufficient to cite a few inftances.

The firft ·is from the addrefs to the fun in Carthon, ' But thofe thyfelf moveft a- ' lone; *who can be· a companion* of thy ' courfe.' The phrafe in Italics is much longer than one would wifh.

The other is from Lathmon ; ' Offian ' rufh'd forward in his ftrength, and the ' people fell before him ; *as the grafs by* ' *the ftaff of the boy, when he whiftles a-* ' *long the field, and the gray beard of the* ' *thiftle falls. But carelefs the youth moves* ' *on; his fteps are towards the defert.*' The fame may be faid of this.

III.

The beft critics of France confefs, that their language, as to found, cadence, and turn of expreffion, is, as they exprefs them-
                                        felves,

felves, extremely profaic, as well as mono-
tonous.

IV.

The poet and all his perfonages are un-
civilized.

This is no proof that a work is bad of
its kind, though it may be true that its
kind is inferior. Mixing much in civilized life, confidering little or not at all any
but the ideas of fuch a ftate of fociety, employing a good deal of time in writing in
thefe ideas, attempting feldom or never to
imitate the ideas of uncultivated life, may
eafily hinder a man from entering into the
feelings of a favage.

V.

V.

The frequency of his fimilies and figured expreffions is infifted on.

The poco piu and poco meno of thefe in their numbers, or in each part, will not be agreed on by writers; the oratory of the North Americans fhows them to be not unnatural to favages; and as the Whites are fuperior to any other breed of human creatures, it is no violent fuppofition, that the oratory of at leaft fome varieties of Whites has been alfo much figured.

VI.

That he has made the fun, moon, and ftars dance the bowling green.

Firft, as to the uniformity of his images, Dr Blair, in one of the beft pieces of cri-

K   ticifm

ticiim we have in any language, has fhown that there is not at all in them that uniformity that has been alledged. The number of objects employed is fmall ; but they are placed in many different views.

Next, as to the propriety of them, Dr Blair, in the above mentioned differtation, has feen all that was to be faid on this fubject. The ufe of an image is to make an effect greater than a plain narration would do ; and they have often been employed with approbation, where, I confefs, I could fee no other effect than bringing to reft the excited imagination. It is, therefore, indifpenfible that their effect fhould be of the fame kind or fpecies with that of the object to which they are fubjoined ; but, if this is obferved, it is obvious, and authorifed by univerfal practice, that a confiderable latitude may be allowed in the refemblance. Two inftances will fhow that Offian's images rarely fail in this point : ' *As roll a* ' *thoufand waves to the rock, fo Swaran's* ' *hoft*

‘ *hoſt came on ;*’ Fing. B. 1. ‘ *Nor my ſoul*
‘ *careleſs as that ſea which lifts its blue*
‘ *waves to every wind ;*’ Oethona.

On the latitude allowed in frequency or
in ſtructure of images, I have ſaid above
all I need ſay here.

The principal circumſtance is the ideas
preſented to the mind.

VII.

The want of verſiſication in the Engliſh
appears as a defect of the firſt magnitude.
The principal parts of a piece are much
improved by good verſiſication, which alſo renders the inferior parts more agreeable or leſs tireſome ; beſides, that there is
more difficulty overcome.

There is certainly a pleaſure in ſeeing
difficulty overcome ; this circumſtance,
how-

however, ought not to be put in competition with any difference worth mentioning
in the other articles.

Good verfification has certainly an effect
of the fame kind with imagery; yet, not-
withftanding the licenfe permitted to increafe the concifenefs, is the whole in capital paffages often equal to what might
be attained, with lefs labour, in profe,
where one has fo much more choice? And
is not the effect oftener miffed? I think
that, with regard to the more conftrained
kinds of verfification, as the Italian, he-
roic ftanza, French and Englifh epic verfe,
with rhymes, the matter is very clear. The
ftrict form of the ftanza and the rhymes
are remains of thofe monkifh and Gothic
delicacies which are now every where a-
bandoned, they are of the fame fpecies or
effect with the others, differing only in degree.

It

It is a real lofs, that the clofe of the ftanza and the return of the rhyme, fhould be perceived ; yet they generally obtrude themfelves. This conftraint and labour, therefore, is fubmitted to for a found that, at beft, fhould not be heard, but whofe ufual operation is leffening the effect. Even in Englifh blank verfe it is a lofs that the end of the line fhould be perceived merely as the end of the line *. The effects of a great-er choice are perhaps ftill lefs to be difpenfed with in inferior paffages. This directs us to an irregular verfification, which has more advantage from found than that ftrictly re-gular, and in which, at the fame time, the writer has much more choice. But, tho' fuch verfe has more advantage from found than either regular verfe or profe, yet the latter has ftill fomewhat more choice. As to the preference, this I prefume is like all other cafes of matters of tafte, where

there

---

* The obfervation of Blair (Crit. Diff. on Off.) is al-fo juft, though the Englifh copy be fuppofed the origi-nal.

there are oppofite advantages, that a confiderable latitude muft be admitted. (Vide
Hume on fimplicity and Refinement.)

It were proper, in thefe critics who think
that the being in profe makes fo much a-
gainft the Englifh copy, to fufpend their
judgment of the Galic copy in this refpeƈt,
till it appear.

The opinions anfwered above may appear extremely fuperficial ; fuch as they
are, however, they have determined emi-
nent men. It may feem trifling to wifh
that a capital paffage of Taffo (for inftance) was put into *fuch* French profe as
the opening of Fingal chofe, as being fee-
ble, is put into, in the *Queftions fur l'En-
cyclopedie, article, Anciens et Modernes.*

VIII.

VIII.

The author has not evaded minute ſtrokes, as the author of Phalaris's Epiſtles has done, but enters into painting as minute as any in moſt works, and has preſerved the utmoſt conſiſtency in the painting.

IX.

Blair obſerved, that the imagery is drawn from a few objects, all of uncultivated life, which are placed in ſeveral different lights; that this invention is of great ability; it is quite conſiſtent with the ſavage ſtate; it is ſo different from the practice of poliſhed ages, it was very unlikely to enter into the head of a man in our times; there is no deviation into civilized life; the attempt is bold and executed with ſuccefs, though a great quantity of imagery is far

beyond

beyond what is ufed in civilized times, and extremely various.

X.

Whatever grounds for the mythology might have been found in the High-lands, there is none refembling it in books, only fome ftrokes in the Old Teftament, a book not likely to be taken for a model.

Milton's failure . in that his devils, angels, and the Almighty, are but men, if one or two ftrokes on Satan be not excepted, had indeed not been obferved *, but the charaꞓer of the age is not favour-able, either to the produꞓion or reception of mythology. The charaꞓer he had to affume was extremely favourable to both. But he faw that, in the fublime, there is indiftinꞓnefs. All the various and nume-

rous

* I have no where met this remark ; but I think it requires only being made, to be admitted. ·

rous paintings are amazingly executed, and
in the fimplicity of a favage of great genius.

XI.

Blair has obferved another circumftance
which ftrongly marks times greatly more
rude than ours. ' No artful tranfitions;
' nor full and extended connection of
' parts; fuch as we find among the po-
' ets of later times, when order and
' regularity of compofition were more
' ftudied and known; but a ftile al-
' ways rapid and vehement; in narration
' concife, even to abruptnefs, and leaving
' feveral circumftances to be fupplied by the
' reader's imagination.' Every one would
not notice it, and very few could fupport
it.

L.   XII.

XII.

The want of abſtract ideas, ſo deciſive a mark of rude times, did not eſcape the acute obſervation of Blair. Though Condamine's voyage was printed many years before M'Pherſon's firſt publication, yet there was no mean ſagacity in making uſe of it. It is extremely difficult to abſtain from theſe through the whole length of ſuch a work ; yet this is done in ſuch a manner that the whole lies within the imagination of a Peruvian, in whoſe language, ſays Condamine, though it admits, in a great degree, energy and elegance, there is no word to expreſs *Time, Duration, Space, Being, Subſtance, Matter, Body, Virtue, Juſtice, &c.*

XIII.

XIII.

We cannot but admire the talents that could fupport, as he has done, through fo large a work, the character of a great fa-vage poet, painting, minutely, in the fhac-kles of an imagery, a train of compofition, and an extent of idea fo different from thofe of civilized times, let him write ever fo much at his eafe, but ftill more if he was difturbed by confcioufnefs of deceit, or o-ther occupations *.

The queftion comes, then, whether his other writings fhow poetical and hiftorical talents equal to fuch a performance?

On it I fhall fay nothing.

If

* Alzire is a great work ; but the Indians are more Europeans than Peruvians. There is only one article in which they refemble the favages, that their paffions are fomewhat lefs reftrained than the others. Yet the parts of the Peruvians muft have been confidered by the au-thor, as one of, if not the gr(ateft novelty in the piece.

If it were made to appear that he who could fit down ferioufly to write the preface, the notes, the differtation on the antiquity of Offian, and of that before the fecond volume, and the introduction to the hiftory of Britain and Ireland, (this laft was publifhed fome years after Offian) could not have, in hiftory, the acutenefs that appears in the poems, it muft be admitted, either that he did not compofe the poems, or that he underwrote the other pieces to cover the deceit. This laft fuppofition will feem the more bold, if it appears that one genius runs through thefe pieces.

If it appears that the preface, the notes, and the above mentioned differtations, are written as if the author of them did not, in regard to hiftory, underftand the poems, the fame alternative occurs.

If it is made to appear that the poetry he wrote before, or at the time Offian was handed about, is fuch that it could not be
ferioufly

ſeriouſly written by the author of Oſſian,
the ſame alternative occurs. The ſuppo-
ſition, that this was underwritten with a
view to the other, is the more bold the
longer the interval between the appearance
of both, particularly if, when the firſt appeared, the author was ſtriving to get himſelf into notice.

XIV.

Suppoſing, now, for a moment, that
there was an original compoſed in the firſt
ages of Chriſtianity, and that this ſhould,
in all ſucceeding times, have been eſteem-
ed the principal work in the language:
From ignorance, affectation, neglect, and
the numberleſs accidents to which tradi-
tional pieces, ever ſo much repeated, and
perhaps, too, from changes in language,
this muſt have come to Mr M'Pherſon's
hands more or leſs altered, and in different
ways. How much it is difficult to ſay.
This

This renders fingle words or lines a very uncertain foundation for conjecture : Vaftly more uncertain in this cafe than in volumes of law, which ferve as a rule to the countries they are compofed in, which are never trufted to tradition, and which come into the prefs as foon as printing is tolerably done. If it renders the detection of a deceit more difficult, it may caufe an appearance of deceit, though there fhould be none,

XV.

In compofing fuch a work, one who had much lefs confidence in his own powers than was neceffary for attempting the Enlifh copy of Offian, (not to mention the Gaelic copy he would expect would be called for) might naturally enough think of fetting it up againft Homer: Yet there is not one attempt at wit in the whole collection,

lection, not even at the pleasantry of a
melancholy bard.

XVI.

The generosity of Fingal and others is
much insisted on. I inquired so late what
opportunity I had, and made so little use
of what I had; that I can only say, that
M'Pherson is not the first who represented
Fingal sparing his enemies.

XVII.

It has been said there is chivalry in the
poems.

By chivalry is meant here, that refined
chivalry which has been painted in so many histories and romances.

This,

This, with the five following objections,
if admitted, would go far to prove, that
very little of the work was fabricated by
M'Pherson; the more, if they are errors
in the ftrain of the notes, &c. They are
all blunders not eafily fufpeded of the ar-
tifice which fabricated the poems; for,
though every man has weak moments, e-
very man revifes, and deceit caufes anxiety.
But thefe objections, it is to be confeffed,
are not well founded.

Chivalry muft have come gradually and
flowly to its height; all origins, fays He-
naut, are obfcure. We know not in whofe,
or in how many countries, its coarfe be-
ginnings appeared; whether many countries had not to learn from foreigners, becaufe thefe were entirely given up, or that
they remained the fame, or that they were
improved fo flowly. Here the defiring and
obtaining fingle combats, or combats of
numbers againft numbers, for mere name,

the

the wifhing to be remembered after death
to a wife or a young woman, are given,
even in Englifh, in fuch a manner, that
they at moft only refemble what we may
conceive chivalry, in its rudeft ftate, to
have been, and very different from what
it afterwards came to be. Infifting that
this alfo is done by M‘Pherfon, fuppofes
that he thoroughly underftood chivalry; an
addition which will be allowed to be at
leaft too confiderable to be dropt.

Befides the chance there was of variations prior to M‘Pherfon, I heard a poem repeated, containing combats of numbers againft numbers, and fingle combats,
which was certainly not compofed by
M‘Pherfon.

XVIII.

Here appears a Therfites. M‘Pherfon
was not the firft who prefented him. In the

M   only

only poem I could repeat of the few I ever
heard, Connan (the Therfites) defires Fingal to put into his hands a perfon defign-
ed by the word we at prefent tranflate King,
whom Fingal had fpared, after vanquifh-
ing him in fingle combat, that he might take
off his head.

XIX.

Cuchullin has a chariot *. It is to be obferved, that none of the others ufe one;
and he appears only in Ireland. I know
that M'Pherfon was not the firft who gave
a defcription of Cuchullin's chariot.

XX.

Mr Gibbon has fhowed that there is little reafon to think that Offian knew the
name

---

* Dio (Xiph. lib. 76.) fays the Caledonians, in the
age of Severus, had horfes, and fought in chariots.

name Caracalla. In fabricating the poems, it would be natural to affign, within certain limits, the time they were written in. This would, however, be equally natural in very many of thofe who tranfmitted, either by writing or repetition, genuine poems. There is no man but would examine a little the paffages he inferted, for this purpofe. The few books requifite for the hiftory of Caracalla were at M'Pherfon's hand, and the hiftory of the name is no way difficult. Father Bower could not avoid giving circumftances ; but the neceffity here was not at all fo great as to force one to infert what was fcarcely poffible, and not at all probable ; for it is very eafily feen, that the want of fuch a particular would not weigh much among the other evidence, external and internal.

My information is fo flender, that I only know that there is mention, in traditions, of the Son of the King of the World ; I know

not

not whether he is an imaginary perfonage,
or whether he is not even given as fuch.

XXI.

In the Differtation on the Antiquity, &c.
of Offian's Poems, and in the notes, Caros
is faid to be the fame as Caraufius, and Ca-
racul is fuppofed to be Caracalla. Fingal
oppofed him about the year 210. Ofcar,
fay 70 years after, oppofed Caraufius, who
affumed the purple A. D. 287. Fingal
furvived Ofcar, (Temora, B. 1.); and,
though, he felt the effects of age fo much,
that he then declared he was to fight
the laft of his fields, yet he appears ftill
far fuperior to all the heroes ; and that in
favage life, in fuch a country, and fuch a
climate.

!XXII.

XXII.

There is in Carthon a ftrange error. Fin-gal, in a very fuperior piece of poetry, fym-pathifes with Cleffamor that Balclutha was defolate. As foon as Carthon's veffels ap-pear, he is known to be the King of Bal-clutha; the bard fpeaks to him by his name. In his anfwer, he gives himfelf as the heir of thofe whofe dwelling Comhal had de-ftroyed; he is young. Balclutha is placed on the Clyde; Fingal muft have been known in, and had fome knowledge of thefe quarters; for, (not to mention the fpoils of the Roman conquefts, and that M'Pherfon, in a note to the war of Caros, places Hidallan's country in or near Stirling-fhire) Comhal and Cleffamor had made in-curfions into the country feized by the Ro-mans; Ofcar had gone to the neighbour-hood of the Romans; Fingal had fought againft them oftener than once, and was

juft

juſt returned from an incurſion. It is need-
leſs to ſay how much Cleſſamor's affections
were ſtill engaged by what had happened
at Balclutha. Yet Cleſſamor goes down
without any queſtions being aſked by himſelf, or any one elſe, or the leaſt ſuſpicion
being expreſſed, that Carthon might be his
ſon or near relation. Carthon is a work
of much enthuſiaſm; but the error is not
only very groſs, but of a ſpecies M'Pherſon was not likely to fall into. In the bard
it was impoſſible. It is to be accounted for
moſt naturally by M'Pherſon's keeping to
what he found.

XXIII.

It is with a good deal of diffidence I enter upon the ſpecimen of the original ſub-
joined to the Engliſh copy. One who
hears the language conſtantly, and hears
little in it he can ſtudy with pleaſure, may,
if he is a man of habit, feel a mechanical
averſion

averfion to any new thing that appears in
it. I applied to a clergyman in my neigh-
bourhood, a man of tafte, who faid he was
alfo of opinion that the Englifh copy was
fuperior to the Gaelic.

The Gaelic copy feems to me amazingly
contrived to fupport the deceit. That mode
of compofition which, as Blair obferved,
marks times greatly more rude than ours,
is carried ftill further in the Gaelic, though
in verfe, than in the profe in Englifh. The
whole is more concife, too, in fome meafure, no doubt, from the nature of the language. In many capital paffages, this
makes the Gaelic copy prodigioufly fuperior. I cannot fay, (I am, indeed, no good
judge) I have feen above two or three
words that feemed Englifh, nor any terms
of phrafe peculiar to Fnglifh. If the Gaelic was really the original, it is ftrange that
there fhould be nothing of this: Some
might remain, though fome were corrected.

In

In tranflating fuch an original as the Gaelic, the hand of a civilized tranflator could not but fome appear, more or lefs; *Via. Piercy's Rio Verde.*

It feems to me, that the two copies are not farther from, or nearer to one another, than is perfectly confiftent with the fuppofition of the Englifh being a tranflation from the Gaelic, done by a mafterly hand.

XXIV.

Comes Littoris Saxonici is an office of the firft ages of our aera. The Littus Saxonicum per Britanniam lies in the fouth of the ifland, and the other on the coaft of Gaul, oppofite to the fouthern part of Britain.

XXV.

He fays little of obfolete expreffion in his original ; the language of the fpecimen he gives, and of courfe, the whole, to a trifle at moft, is intelligible at this day, to all who underftand Gaelic unmixed with Englifh. This I know is the cafe with other poems to which the name of Offian is put.

Though the general mechanifm of human paffion is every where the fame ; yet the particular differences are numerous and confiderable, as alfo their effects.

It may eafily have happened, among the various tracts which language takes, that, in a bad country, feldom quiet, where conqueft or religion affected the language but little, where foreign models were not imitated, but rather difliked ; and where there was fome attachment to anceftors, fome time after a language had got into the form we call grammatical, it might remain long while the people continued

N   rude,

rude, without much alteration in the words
or ſtructure.

Attempts at elegance, ſo minute as to affect the words and ſtructure of the language, ſuppoſes a degree of refinement.

Though this conjecture ſeems ſo ſafe,
that it may appear to be what has generally happened among nations in ſuch circumſtances, yet the fact may paſs unno-
ticed; the mere language of people in bar-
bariſm does not tempt civilized nations to
make dictionaries of it; and among themſelves, when once books, even tranſlations,
become tolerably numerous, a more minute
elegance is ſtudied ; foreign books are ſtudied, and then nothing but a moſt obſtinate
attachment can hinder the language from
changing very much, though it ſhould be
affected neither by religion nor conqueſt.
Books and records ſecure to us the knowledge of the language in all its variations,
and an alteration may be imagined ſo rapid

as that they would retard it. But it is not probable that fuch an alteration ever happened while a people was ftill barbarous and left to themfelves.

In the cafe in queftion, the only alteration that I have heard has taken place of late, is the intermixture of Englifh; if we go but a little way back, we can hardly fuppofe that they aimed at elegance fo minute as to affect much the words or the conftruction of the language.

It does not feem probable that the bards have, for feveral centuries paft, had rank enough to get their changes followed, if they were to propofe any. If we go ftill farther back, we may fairly fuppofe them to have had lefs inclination to make any. If a chieftain had any whimfical inclination to change, he would expect little encouragement from the neighbouring tribes.

But

*   *   *   *

But there are also some confiderations which favour the fufpicion that M'Pherfon is the author.

XXVI.

If they had been compofed in the High-lands, within thefe two or three centuries, they would have been forced into the notice of the public as Hardyknute and Row-ley's poems, as they would have been compofed merely to draw attention. The times before that, Blair has well obferved, were lefs favourable to fuch a production than the ftate of fociety reprefented in them. Now, in fome refpects, they may feem not fuch as we would expect to be done in fuch times.

Scarce any degree of judgment is e-nough to hinder men from rating too high the attention due to what has long employ-ed them. The more men are moved by paffion, the more they dwell on minute particulars

particulars connected with the principal object. Savages are lefs apt to ftudy the movements of their minds than civilized men. They have more violent paffion, and from having fewer ideas to diftract them, they dwell the more on what engages them. Hence the minutenefs of Homer's narrative. He tells us when his hero buckles his fhoes and ties his garters; the whole cooking of a feaft; who gets the chine; not only the detail of every combat between the principal perfonages, but the wound by which a hero kills every obfcure perfon is given, and with great ftudy of words. It is now infupportable, and would be fo, though favages were not the fubject. Not to mention the lift of the forces, Taffo's combats are now tafk-reading. Nothing of all this is in Offian; the perfonages are prefented only in fuch light as to intereft us; no more particulars than are, in our eyes, enough to complete the impreffion: They cannot tire, ftill lefs difguft any one who can bear favages at all.

XXVII.

The landfcapes are numerous, and done by a mafter; yet many, not to fay moft of thefe ftrokes are of a kind, one is tempted to imagine, would have little effect on a favage, even a bard who drew his fimilies from inanimate objects, and ftill lefs on his hearers, though they are not the landfcapes of civilized times. For inftance, ' I came ' to the place where Fillan fought; nor ' voice nor found is there. A broken hel-' met lay on earth; a buckler cleft in ' twain. Where, Fillan, where art thou, ' young chief of echoing Morven? He ' heard me leaning againft a rock, *which* ' *bent its gray head over the ftream.*' He ' heard; but, fullen, dark, he ftood;' Tem. B. 6. The fame may, perhaps, be faid of much of the imagery, not to fay the great-er part of it.

Thefe

Thefe affect the whole book, and in thefe the character of a favage poet may feem to be departed from : They are much more delicate than thofe taken notice of in Sect. 17. 18. 19. 20. 21. 22. They are not more delicate than thofe noticed in fome other fections, and which favour the contrary fuppofition; but it ought not to be forgot, that it is eafy to fee how much the book is improved by them, in the judgment of our times.

* , * * *

There occur fome other confiderations, which though of lefs weight, may feem confiftent with the fame fuppofition.

XXVIII.

I have elfewhere (Paper whether the Attacotti were Cannibals in the time of Jerom) endeavoured to fhow, that it is improbable hunters fhould have iron. Once when I applied it to this cafe, it was anfwered, ‘ They

' They got thefe as the Indians got theirs.'
I have in the fame Paper remarked, that it
is not natural that Hunters fhould fight
chiefly hand to hand, and that the fpear,
fword, and fhield, fhould be their chief
weapons. Yet, though the fhepherd ftate
would furnifh many images and ftrokes
for landfcapes, we find no traces of it here.
It is true I know poems prior to M'Pherfon, wherein the arms and manner of fighting are the fame as here; but not to infift
that the want of imagery in them caufes
a fufpicion of their high antiquity, or that
thefe arms and manner of fighting expofes
themfelves to fufpicion, inftead of helping
to clear the others; the collection printed
by M'Pherfon, though perhaps in no great
proportion to what has paffed under Offian's name, is ftill large as well as various.
I recollect but three, befides the allufions
to the fteeds. Thefe laft are not decifive,
as they are very few, and the denomina-
tion ' Steeds of the ftranger's land,' is fometimes ufed. Of the others, the fcene of
that

that in the firſt and that in the ſecond book
of Fingal, is in Ireland, the third is in
Caric-Thura, perhaps the moſt ſuſpicious
of all the poems. .

XXIX.

It ſeems ſtrange that Oſſian ſhould have
made his own father, who was for ſome
time his own contemporary, threaten and
worſt the ſpirit of Loda. It is true he was,
as Blair remarks, the divinity of another
and a hoſtile people ; but Homer placed
his ſtory in remote times. Notwithſtand-
ing the excellent inſinuation in the laſt note,
that Oſſian thought the Gods deſerved what
they might meet with for interfering in our
affairs, the error might eaſily eſcape notice
in the enthuſiaſm of compoſing ſo great a
work as Carric-Thura. The note at the
cloſe ſuppoſes there are precedents for it.
Some things here may ſeem imitations of

O   the

the Old Teſtament, and ſet up againſt Homer.

XXX.

Temora.

In Fingal the ſucceſſion of heroes is ſo natural, (whatever may be thought of the epiſode of Lamderg and Ullen in the 5th book,) as to extend the piece with as great propriety as can eaſily be imagined. But here Fingal had loſt Oſcar in the beginning, yet ſtill keeps off, though a moſt obſtinate reſiſtance was to be expected, and a long ſucceſſion is preſented. The error cannot be called a groſs one ; particularly, if the ſeven books were written after the bewitching ſucceſs of the firſt volume. But Oſſian could not deviate much from fact in what had happened ſo recently, however he might colour.

O N

ACCOMPANYMENT.

ACCOMPANYMENT.

I ENTER only into a part of the fubject. I hope, however, what I fay will be of ufe to fome of thofe who can make experiments. I do not attempt to afcertain how the parts influence one another. This, among other things, requires a very nice ear. D'Alembert did not truft his own fo far as to enter into the facts which were difputed, when he wrote, (and which, for aught I know, are fo ftill) though they were fo material.

If any part in a harmony is once fixed, whether it be the firft, the fecond, the bafs, or any other accompanyments, it regulates all the others within narrower or wider limits, whatever be the principles which guide the compofition; and the choice of thefe principles does not oblige the compofer to begin with one part in preference to another. I fhall confider only pieces compofed on the principles of Rameau and thofe of Tartini (Romieu's tract I have not feen) and the very fimpleft cafes.

D'Alembert grounds Rameau's fyftem on two facts. The firft, that, if a ftring is founded, we hear, befides its found, the octave of its fifth above, and the double octave of its greater third above. The fecond, that, inftead of any note, its octave above or below may be fubftituted with little variation in the effect, and that it will make but little difference to fink or raife the whole piece an octave *.

Suppofe,

* This fact is not true. Not to dwell on greater variations, it is eafy to produce an inftance, where, by
finking

. Suppofe, now, thefe facts true, and that they alone influence compofition.

Confider, firft, a melody compofed by one who had no idea of the fundamental bafs, and which has been firft ufed without any bafs ; fuch melodies, it is well known, exift in great numbers.

What regulates this melody ?

To this it is anfwered, that, fince it is agreeable, it muft have one fundamental bafs,

finking a whole piece an octave, it becomes a burlefque from being good. One reafon of the error may be, that, from its refemblance, the octave fo fubftituted fuggefts to certain ears the note. (V. Hume's inquiry on human underftanding.) I enter not here further into this fact, though it were not hard ; for I find in Rouffeau's dictionary, article *Harmony*, that Mr Elévé of the Montpellier Society had fhowed, that, ' beginning by this fact, ' there was nothing demonftrated, or even fully eftablifh- ' ed ' in the whole fyftem ; and this treatife I have neither feen, nor met with any one who had.

bafs, or more, and that bafs regulates the melody *·

The next queftion is, what regulates this fundamental bafs ? in its key ? in the pitch it is to fet out on ? its firft note ? its progrefs to the clofe ? and the clofe ?

What fuits the melody beft, in regard to thefe, is chofe as its fundamental bafs †.

Suppofe

---

* Though I confefs I do not underftand what D'A-lembert means by his propofition, that ‘ melodie nait ‘ de la harmonie,’ yet this anfwer feems to me the only one confiftent with his writings.

† What is propofed in D'Alembert's writings is to fhow, that, to every piece there is a fundamental bafs, fuch, that notes in the upper parts, whether one or more, are allowed or not according as they fuit it on the prin-ciples mentioned above. This certainly is not done; but I, enter not into that queftion, becaufe of Eftévé's treatife; from the ftrain of Jamard's and Rouffeau's books, I am (perhaps too eafily) tempted to think this is the only fubject of it. A choice of fundamental baffes is evidently fuppofed. If the above ftated principles are the only which influence compofition, my propofition would go ftill further, if it

be

Suppofe, next, the fundamental bafs fixed firft, and a melody compofed from it ; this is certainly practicable.

In this cafe, the fundamental bafs regulates, within certain limits, the melody.

The mufic may ftill be the very fame, whichever of the two the compofer choofes fhould regulate the other.

Suppofe the fundamental bafs made firft. A note fixed, and in confequence its feventeenth major fet down in the melody becaufe of its found. with the bafs, and becaufe the bafs is ac.ompanied by another feventeenth major and a twelfth. If the

P   me-

be true, what I think very clear, that, in the fundamental bafs, there is no rule of fucceffion but its connection with the upper parts fixed before it; and that thefe parts, though they might bear to it a conftant relation, are not fixed by that, but by their relation to one another, at the fame time, that it is proper to remark the former relation alfo.

melody is made firſt, the ſame note fixed
as is placed in the other melody, the very
ſame conſiderations give the ſame baſs, the
ſeventeenth major below; becauſe of its
own ſound, and that it generates a note
the uniſon of the upper note beſides its
twelſth. And ſo on.

Conſider, next a part betwixt the two,
ſay a ſecond.

Suppoſe the fundamental baſs made firſt.
The ſecond its twelfth, and the upper part
its ſeventeenth major, becauſe it generates
their uniſons, and bec——ʰ of their agree-
ment with one another. If the ſecond is
firſt made, the ſame note fixed in it as in
the former caſe, the ſame reaſons of choice
give the fundamental baſs and upper part
the ſame. If the upper part is firſt made,
the ſame reaſons give the two other parts
the ſame. And ſo on.

The ſame of all the other parts that are
added.

Tartini

Tartini forms the bafs, by the harmony
a chord makes with its aliquot parts, and
the attention due to the third tone gene-
rated by two founding together. In his
Trattato di Mufica, chap. 1. is the following paffage : ' Mi domandera poi ella in
' fecondo luogo in qua relazione fi trovi
' quefto terzo fuono agl'intervalli rifpettivi
' da quali rifulta. Le rifpondo che dati i
' feguenti intervalli, de quali e rifpettivo
' terzo fuono il fottopofto, quefto fara di-
' monftrativamente il baffo armonico de
' dati intervalli e fara paralogifmo qualun-
' que altro baffo vi fi fottoponga.'

&c.

Suppofe now of the firft three notes *mi* and
do fharp given, and that the bafs *la* is fixed

from

from them, becaufe it is unifon of the tone
they generate. If the upper part *mi* and
the bafs *la* were given, and that the fame
confideration were to guide, this fixes the
fecond upper part *do* fharp, becaufe that is the
note which, with the fixed upper part *mi*,
generates the unifon of the bafs. And fo
on.

And the fame reafoning may be applied,
though the compofition were guided by
the principles employed by D'Alembert and
thofe of Tartini together ; or any others.

But what part ought to be firft made * ?

Surely that part to which all the others
ferve as accompanyments, more particularly, if the effect is to be produced more by
the

---

* It is known to compofers that it ought not be attempted to carry on the part without a view, more or
lefs, to the others, though it could be done ; and that it
cannot be done though attempted, becaufe any part fuggefts the others more or lefs.

the fucceffion of notes, and lefs by harmony. We can the lefs expect meaning, if
the beginning is made by an accompanyment inftead of that part ; and ftill the lefs
according as the part begun by, is propofed
to have lefs feeling.

If one were to compofe a .piece of mufic,
in which the bafs were the principal part
in the expreffion, there would be the fame
propriety in beginning by it, as there is
now in beginning by the upper: As alfo,
in beginning by any other part which is
made the principal in the expreffion. This
will probably be tried one day ; at prefent
it appears not fo natural.

I fhall endeavour to explain how.

High notes (to fpeak in the inaccuracy
of common language) fill the ear more than
the low.

Here,

Here, as in other things, the females have invented little ; their voice pleafes us more than our own, and is an octave high-er.

The only other animals who appear to us to have mufic, arc birds ; their pipe is acute, and pleafes us.

As making the bafs an accompanyment feems to me not to have been done from mere caprice, I imagine that this, and fuch other things, will be tried, and come into ufe, chiefly from the love of novelty and variety.

O F

OF THE

EXISTENCE of BODY.

EXISTENCE of BODY.

THE exiftence of body muft always be taken for granted: Reafonings on it are to be made only to difcover the nature of our frame.

It is faid that there has been difcovered an argument, which admits no anfwer, to fhow the exiftence of body an abfurdity.

I prefume, that an argument, or any thing like an argument, to prove that body does not exift, is entirely out of our power.

Does body exift ?

Q

The

The firſt queſtion in this inquiry is, whether the mind perceives body?

This point has been made very clear. Sextus Empiricus, (*Sceptical Suppoſitions, B. 2.
c. 7. and elſewhere ; alſo Adverſ. Mathemat.
l. 7. § Of Man*). Berkley, (*Dialog. on Body*).
And, ſtill more, DAVID HUME, (*Trea-
tiſe of Human Nature, Vol. 1. and Eſſay on
the Sceptical Philoſophy*), have ſhewed, beyond diſpute, that body is never preſent to
the mind : That nothing is ever preſent to
the mind but ſenſations, as extenſion, colour, ſolidity, &c. alledged to be impreſſions made on our frame by body ; movements of our frame alledged to be cauſed
by body.

The next queſtion is, whether theſe ſenſations or perceptions are impreſſions made
on our frame by body, placed without it,
or not ?

Sextus

Sextus Empiricus, loc. cit. (and HUME, loc. citat.) have fhowed, that it is out of our power to form any thing like an argument to prove that they are caufed by body. The mind never perceives body; nothing beyond thefe fenfations: There is no poffibility of attaining any experience what may be beyond them.

The fame reafoning fhows that it is e-qually out of our power to prove that they are not caufed by fomething without us.

Accordingly, I prefume it not difficult to difcover the fallacy of any reafoning which pretends to eftablifh that point, or the contrary, let us examine the celebrated reafoning of Berkley.

It is proved, and admitted, fays he, that the fecondary qualities of body, as colour, tafte, &c. exift only in the mind, and have no prototype; in the fame manner, it may be proved, that the primary qualities, ex-

tenfion

tenfion and folidity, exift alfo only in the mind, and reprefent no prototype: Now, fince we know nothing of body but qualities, and that all qualities exift only in the mind; it is a contradiction to fay that body can exift, except in the mind.

' *Extenfion and folidity, as well as the* ' *other qualities of body, fuch as colour, &c.* ' *exift only in the mind.*'

He has proved, that extenfion, colour, &c. are movements of our frame, alledged to be caufed by body. This is clearly afcertained to be his meaning; the proof is long, perfpicuous, and minute.

' *Since all the qualities of body exift only* ' *in the mind, it is a contradiction to fay* ' *that body exifts but in the mind.*'

This is juft, if by qualities of body is meant movements, fuppofed to be of body,
which

which produce extenfion, colour, and thefe other movements of our frame.

His argument therefore is, Extenfion, colour, &c. are movements of our frame; fince the movements which produce thefe are not movements of external body, but movements of our frame, fuppofing body to exift, is fuppofing body incapable of caufing extenfion, folidity, &c. or, in common language, body, which has no qualities, a flat contradiction. This reafoning requires no long commentary. There is no attempt to fhow whether the movements of our frame are caufed by movements of body or not; but, relying on an expreffion of common language, (qualities of body) which was not even invented with any view to this inquiry, he fees no diftinction betwixt the movements of our frame, extenfion, colour, &c. and the movements of body, or of our frame which produce them.

Nor

Nor is there any thing like an argument to fupport his conclufion, in which ever of the two fenfes, above mentioned, we take his phrafe, ' qualities of body.'

He proves that extenfion, colour, &c. are movements of our frame. The next queftion is, Whether thefe are caufed by body, placed without it or not ? Into this queftion he never entered.

If thefe are not caufed by movements of body, it is plainly a contradiction, an ab-furdity to fay that body exifts beyond our frame. He never attempted to prove that they were not, as I have juft remarked, though his treatife is very minute.

It cannot be pretended, that if extenfion and folidity, &c. are admitted to be only movements of our frame, it follows plain-ly and palpably, that they are caufed by nothing external *. That is not to be admitted

---

* Citing parallel cafes is very bad reafoning; it is, however,

ted without a proof; no proof has hitherto been attempted; and where are the
grounds of it to be looked for?

To make a proof, he fhould have fhowed that extenfion, colour, &c. were only
movements of our frame, and that thefe
were not caufed by body placed without it.
His inference would then have been juft.

' *Exift only in the mind*,' is a .very improper expreffion ; but if, inftead of it,
movements of our frame, or any fuch expreffion had been ufed, the doubt would
have more readily have occurred, whether
thefe were the effect of any thing external.
' *Qualities*

however, fo often ufed, that one is inclined to fufpect it
may fometimes have its ufe: I fhall, therefore, venture it
for once. A piece of ice becomes fluid on coming near a
heated body. The fluidity in the water is a diftinct thing
from the heat that comes from the body without it. The
fluidity exifts only in the water, to ufe Berkley's language,
and has no prototype. Does it, therefore, follow, that
it neither is nor can be caufed by any thing external?

' *Qualities of body*' is a very convenient expreſſion for the purpoſe it was invented; but it was not invented with any view to this inquiry. It is here very improper, the ſubject has been thought by many not the very eaſieſt to comprehend; this expreſſion could not but make it leſs eaſy. But if he had ſpoke clear language, uſed inſtead of that phraſe, either *movements of our frame, ſuppoſed to be cauſed by movements of body,* or *movements of body, ſuppoſed to cauſe them,* or uſed theſe two as ſynonimous terms, the fallacy of the reaſoning had been ſoon diſcovered.

' We *know* nothing of body but quali-
' ties;' either of the two expreſſions uſed by Sextus Empiricus, ' *the mind has*
' *no intercourſe* with external things,' or
' *the ſenſe ſhows to the mind,* not. external
' things, but its own feeling,' or any other analogous expreſſion, would alſo have more readily ſuggeſted a doubt than that he uſes.
That

That part of his argument where he
fhows that extenfion and folidity are mere
movements of the frame, as well as colour,
&c. is well; but, I apprehend it is not eafy
to point out any attempt more defective
than the reft.

R

OBSERVATIONS

ON

FORTIFICATIONS

WITH

REVETED DITCHES,

WHERE THE

WORKS ARE RAISED IN AMPHITHEATRE.

DEDICATION.

Oh curas hominum ! Oh quantum eſt in rebus inane!

THE opinions in the following fheets were formed long before they were put into writing. I kept them by me for fome time, and I print them now much againſt my will, merely becaufe of an accident which left me anfwerable for their errors, and would have transferred any merit they had. The firſt treatife ſtood originally in lefs than a page, and had no figures; but having feen that no reputation or capacity could fecure a man from being charged with the moſt vulgar errors, I found myfelf forced to fpread it: I added, too, fome applications of its principles. The fecond was, from the fame reafon, made from the firſt, much longer than I could have wiſhed. In thefe circumſtances, it is furely very unpleafant to me, who have never ferved, to print on military fubjects; but, at leaſt, I am not obliged to inquire whether heaven is defended by infinite artillery, or whether the devil charged in column.

PREFACE.

IF in any inquiry of fact and exiftence we afk whether we have gone all the length poffible, we can hitherto fatisfy ourfelves by no other expedient than an examination of every attempt to add to our knowledge; nor do we know whether any other ever fhall or can be found. But have we any reafon to think, that, in the military fciences, we are advanced fo far as to have any thing like a ground to put the queftion? All appearances fay quite the contrary. In the civil fciences, as the mind, chemiftry, botany, difcoveries are every day made; and thefe, inftead of narrowing the fubjects of inquiry, have hitherto extended them, and that regularly the further as each ftep is gained; to fuch a pitch too. Nor is this opinion of them peculiar to me, but will be affented to by every

S   one

one converfant in thefe fubjects, with fo
little hefitation, that they would not give
the opinion,. or even the doubt, whether
we were near our laft ftage in them, the
name of fcepticifm. Indeed, if ever we
fhall attain the utmoft our frame permits,
in fome of thefe fciences, it is poffible, or
probable if you will, that we may reach it,
in fome a good deal fooner than in others:
But it is ftill unknown, whether we fhall
ever be able to gain that height in any one;
it is equally unknown, whether, though it
were attained, men could ever prove they
had done fo. There is no reafon for thinking that we have already reached this point
in the military fciences, if the others are
in the ftate they feem to be; for we have
no reafon to think that our progrefs fhould
be much greater in them than in others.
The progrefs of each of the other fciences
is liable to be retarded by feveral caufes:
So are the military ones. Forms of government and jurifprudence are thofe whofe
hiftory one would expect fhould approach
the

the neareft to that of the military fciences;
are we to believe that the firft is at its utmoft height : Whether the laft is, is a point
fully fettled by the writings of Cocceius
and Blackftone. The progrefs of the civil
fciences has always been whimfical: That
of the military fciences has been at leaft as
whimfical, I think rather more fo. The
military fciences have been cultivated by
men of great abilities. No doubt, there
were heroes and inventors, when men
fought with ftones and clubs, and defended themfelves in huts, dens, or trees but
then, from the time of Guftavus Adolphus
(and we might go further back), there is a
lift of foldiers, whofe names are not mentioned but with veneration: In the others,
there is a very long lift of names which are
mentioned with equal regard: Within that
period, Rapin has been held a great hifto-
rian, and Petty a great financier, and, on
this fo called fcience, no difcovery has ever
been made by a great general, nor by one
who fhowed genius on any other fubject.

O F

REGULAR FORTIFICATIONS.

Of Dry Ditches.

IT is agreed, that such plans as Belidor's second method, or Biffet's fifth, ought not to be used, except where the town is the whole state, as Hamburg; or its last resource, as Magdeburg happened to be in the seven years war*. I shall examine here

such

---

* The reason given for this is, that troops and stores cannot be afforded to garrison them according to their extent, and that, if they are provided only as the simpler methods,

ſuch methods as are uſed where the ſtake is
leſs, in caſes ſuppoſed, a century ago, to happen every day †.

I.

Fig. 1. is Biſſet's eighth method; Fig. 2.
is Biſſet's firſt method. Theſe, it is allowed, admit a very good defence.

Fig.

methods, the defence they make will be little or nothing
better. This reaſoning is good, and fully enough to decide the caſe in hand. It may be applied to works ſtill
ſimpler than thoſe now preferred, at leaſt, in ſome mea-
ſure. I flatter myſelf I have introduced a principle which
goes further.

† It is now thought not proper to fortify all the places
that would have been fortified then. I preſume this
change of opinion has come, from conſidering the uncertainty whether the places would be beſieged, the manoeuvres of armies being performed with much more di-
ſpatch and ſafety than in theſe days, and that it was obſerved it coſt more to fortify and defend a place than to
take it.

Fig. 3. is done from Fig. 1. Fig. 4. from Fig. 2.

Would it not be better to fortify in such methods as the latter?

First is to be considered the uncertainty whether the place may be besieged, and when.

Suppose the difference of expence in the construction bestowed in additional troops and stores for the smaller works, the others being provided in the usual manner; from which is the best defence to be expected?

The covered way, glacis, and field of Nos 3. and 4. may be as well mined as those of the other. I just mention counter approaches, to show I have not forgot them.

It will not be disputed, that the smaller works are still enough to oblige the besieger

to

to go on by regular approaches, and to batter in breach for more or lefs time.

The aim of the garrifon is to put the befieger to as great expence of men and ftores and to make him employ as much time as they can. The fecret of the defence is to hufband the ftrength of the place, fo as to attain thefe ends in the greateft degree.

While both parties are provided, as they have been in the laft wars, after the befieger is mafter of the glacis of fuch plans as Fig. 1. and 2. if he has conducted himfelf with proper caution, whatever men the garrifon can kill him, they cannot hinder him long from entering the body of the place, though they fhould not have fired a fhot, nor made a fally till then. They always ufe a great proportion of their ftores before he can get there, and lofe many men.

Mining

Mining retards the befieger's progrefs to the creft of the glacis, more than the fire and fallies of fuch places; it kills few men.

The additional charge in the more expenfive plan is laid out over the whole enceinte. The befieger has to repair only the demolition he did.

State two places precifely the fame, but the garrifon, artillery, &c. of the one to thofe of the other, as 15 to 10. The additional charge is employed entirely againft the enemy. This is the chief reafon why large places have made fo much better defences than fmall ones: A decagon, *e. g.* Vid. Le Febvre's and Mont. Rozard's tranflation of Antoni's Treatife of Artillery, dated 1780, (I have not feen the original) is garrifoned and provided according to its number of baftions, the hexagon is attacked, perhaps, by the fame force, or at leaft by a force greater in proportion to that it has for its defence.

On

On the whole, I think we may expect the fmaller works will make the better defence.

II.

Let us now confider the works left at their full height in Fig. 3. and 4.

Many have contended that the body of the place ought to be as low as the outworks which cover it.

One reafon much infifted on was, that, when the out-work was ruined, the cannon might be retired into the inner work.

The covered way, ravelin, baftion, glacis of Vouban's firft method, has never yet been fo fully employed as they might advantageoufly be.

T   Another

Another was, that the befieger could ruin the body of the place at the fame time that he ruined the out-works, and while he was yet at a diftance *. In anfwer to this, it has been obferved, that the demolition is not fo great as is reprefented, the mark is fo fmall, and the repair not difficult; that Vouban had not feen a parapet fo ruined that it could not be ufed; and before the befieger begins to batter in breach, the parapet may be put in almoft as good condition as it was the firft day of the fiege: That the command given by the height was of great confequence, particularly when the enemy came near.

What refpects the demolition in this anfwer has the lefs weight, according as the befieger brings on his batteries, (compare Biffet and Le Febvre); on the whole, it appears clearly, that the high line is the beft; but

* One reafon for the numerous batteries we fee in fome methods has fometimes been probably the cafe of the repair.

but the expence of carrying this height round the whole enceinte, would furnifh a great quantity of ftores, if the works are completely reveted; if they are demi-re-veted, the expence ought not to be faved.

As to the curtain, I need only fay, that, in each point, I would wifh to have fome little thing to anfwer the ufe of a cavalier, and that diftance increafes the uncertainty of the aim of mortars, and hobitz ftill more than that of cannon: It feems admitted, that the befieger ought not to take the ra-velin; nor would lowering the curtain to its level make it his intereft to do fo.

III.

Many methods of fortification are fo admirably contrived, that it feems barbarous to attempt to bring them into difufe; if, however, in the courfe of fuch attempts, a wafte of public money is prevented, the

man

man who does it will not be entirely a vegetable in his country, and he cannot be entirely diſſatisfied with the time he has beſtowed on it. I think I ſhould have little pleaſure in conſtructing a fine plan that I ſuppoſed would never have juſtice done to it.

Fig. 5. is done from Pagan's firſt method; it is allowed to admit a very good defence.

It is eaſily ſeen that I do not ſuppoſe the advantage of employing ſtores on the counter-guard, rather than on the baſtion, and any other uſe there is hitherto found in that work, a compenſation for its expence.

Fig. 6. is done from Fig. 5. Fig. 7. from Fig. 3. and Fig. 8. from Fig. 4. ·

Theſe are ſtill enough to oblige the beſieger to go through a regular ſiege; they admit mining equally as the others.

Againſt the general aſſault, early in the ſiege, the flanks of the baſtions, in Fig. 3. and 4. are an excellent defence, which theſe laſt have not. Vaulted batteries, for two or three pieces of cannon, could be made in them at little expence; which, againſt ſuch an aſſault, would be of great uſe. But it would be neceſſary, a little before he began to batter in breach, to take away the guns and ram them as the gallery of a mine.

IV.

Where a fortreſs is done where there were no houſes, there is a vaſt quantity of earth which muſt be carried away; where a place already built is to be fortified, the interval between the buildings and the works affords, almoſt every where, a great deal. Without the works earth is always to be had in the fields, and little heights are often met with that would be of uſe to the beſieger.

V.

V.

On what diminution of the ditch, a material addition muſt be made to the numbers of the garriſon, and what addition on
account of different degrees of diminution,
is what will not be agreed on till many
trials are made. I dare only remark, that,
in a matter ſo uncertain, and ſo important,
nicety is not at preſent to be aimed at, probably never.

VI.

If a gallery in the counter-ſcarp were
to be carried round the whole place, on
account of the reſiſtence made from its
loop-holes to the paſſage of the ditch, the
money muſt be held ill laid out. If there
is one, why make it large?

VII.

VII.

Le Febvre, in his example of a fiege, fuppofes the retrenchment in the baftion made after the fiege is begun; in ftating the queftion how much mining ought to be done beforehand, he gives the mining at Fort Jauernik of Schweidnitz, which he calls Travaux immenfes, (Note, p. 8. *Effai fur les mines*), as works which were not *faites de longue main.* If the excavations made by the globes of compreffion (Plate 3. fiege of Schweidnitz) are admitted as a fcale, (there is no other) the galleries beyond the counter-fcarp were five hundred fathom. I need enter into this queftion no further than to obferve, that though fomething ought always to be done beforehand, the expence of fuch works as are not done till the befieged has fixed where he attacks, is not laid out till wanted, and only where wanted.

MIS-

MISCELLANEOUS REMARKS.

I.

Ought the flank of the baftion to be placed as in Fig. 1. (for inftance), or retired,
as in Fig. 9. or 10.?

Biffet, (Sect. 2. chap. 3. § 56.) fays,
' Bombs are of fo much importance in the
' attack, and anfwer fo effectually all the
' ends which are obtained by counter bat-
' teries of cannon, that there feems to be
' a poffibility of taking fortified towns with
' bombs only*; and, it is certain, that
' there are always more of the cannon of
' the befieged ruined and difmounted by the
' bombs than by the cannon of the enemy,
                                     ' when

---

* There can be no doubt, that a place may be taken
without either cannon or bombs.

' when the former are properly ufed, and
' in abundance.' If retiring the flank of
the baftion made it the befieger's intereft to
lay out fhells againft it, inftead of cannon-
fhot, this is to him fuch a lofs, that the
flank ought to be retired: But merely retiring it does not make that his intereft;
it is, therefore, a matter of indifference.

II.

Though the fize of ditches I propofe
were as proper, as I believe it to be, yet the
imaginations of many will be fo fhocked
by the look of it, that they will not give
the propofal an examination.

Fig. 11. is a ditch twenty fathom wide,
and twelve feet deep. Fig. 12. is twelve
fathoms wide, and eighteen feet deep.

Confidering the great difference of expence, would it not be proper to make

U

them

them as in Fig. 13. and 14. or to flope the
fcarp too, or to flope only the fcarp. Fig.
15. is the body of Fort Jauernick of
Schweidnitz from Le Febvre *. In places
which, by chance, have many troops, fuch
a ditch would be better than thofe in Fig.
11. and 12. A ftair of brick would be
better than reveting the ditch to the top
with brick; but a ftair of brick or ftone
would be fhattered by fhells, and do hùrt
and confufion by the fplinters. Such a compofition as we fee in buildings of the Ro-
mans, if deep enough, would refift fhells
well, and it would not fplinter; but it
would be expenfive †. If there is a gallery
in the counter-fcarp, there is lefs benefit
in this alteration.

III.

* He makes no remark on it.

† Inftead of reveting with ftone, might it not, in fome
fituations, be proper to ufe thefe compofitions.

III.

If the great ditch were continued along the lines of defence, there would be a confiderable portion of it that would not be feen into ; this might in a great meafure be remedied by floping the fcarp towards the flanks and curtain. In the ravelind method, Fig. 16. from the line in which the face of the ravelin produced cuts the ditch, &c. the ground is floped away, fo that the whole ditch is feen into from the flanks and curtain * ; along the foot of thefe there is no excavation. The great faving

---

* I think it needlefs to draw any flopes or communications with the ravelin. I take it to be granted there muft be fome cheap contrivance along the flanks and curtains, for the fake of fallies againft the enemy's lodgements in the ravelin. Other works may alfo be made in the fpace between the lines, &c. at an inconfiderable expence, by finking them fome feet in the ground, as, for inftance, a kind of caponiere, and fomething in the fhape of a redoubt to the ravelin. I enter not here into this matter.

faving that may be made by this I think a very proper one. It may be objected, that the befieger will carry on his attack by taking the ravelin, and thence go to the curtain or fhoulder, and fo find his account more in the attack of this than of Fg. 3. Firft, this place can, on the fame total, be better provided than Fig. 3. by much. In the next place, in attacking Fig. 3. it is not his intereft to take the ravelin ; here taking the ravelin cofts him more than in Fig. 3. Suppofe him now to have made an entry into it, there is next in Fig. 3. the paffage of the great ditch ; here he is more expofed to fuffer by fallies, and the befieged have more opportunity of mining. On the whole, then, it feems the intereft of the befieger to carry on his attack againft the face of the baftion. Even if the two places were equally provided, each in the manner fuitable to its conftruction, but both decently well, this place does not appear much inferior to Fig. 3. The chief difference is, that a practicable breach is eafier

fier made here in the flanks or curtain than
in the faces of the other ; that difference
is in that article very confiderable, but will
not, I prefume, be held to make much difference betwixt the defences, if both are
are equally well conducted *.

IV.

Suppofe the body of the place fortified
by Biffet's eighth method, whether are ravelins to be added, or only common places
of arms in the re-entering angles where the
ravelins ftand †. I think the ravelins well
worth

---

* Long after this was written I was informed by a very good authority at Copenhagen, that fomething like
this has been done in the Belle Croix at Metz (the engineer's name I have forgot) but though the inventor,
whether my informer or the engineer, had printed the
plan, I could not avoid citing his reafoning, if it appeared any way tolerable.

† I ftated the cafe in this manner to avoid entering at
prefent

worth the additional expence. Not becaufe they oblige the befieger to break
ground

prefent into a difcuffion, whether, inftead of the ravelin,
it might not be proper to make only a place of arms of
its fize, (as in Fig. 17.) or inftead of the lunettes in Fig.
2. to make places of arms of their fize, (as in Fig. 18.) or
to zig-zag the covered way otherwife, leaving the great
ditch as ufual. The redoubts have a ftair-cafe like thofe
of the drums of lunettes. The ufe of thefe laft kind of
works is more or lefs as the ftrength of the place is in its
fmall arms or great. Le Febvre informs us, (Siege of
Rivol, chap. 17. laft note) that the drums of the lunettes
at Bergen-op-zoom coft the French dear. Bergen-op-
zoom had an army in it; and there is no one fpot near
at hand but may be made to coft the enemy dear. He
has not faid but it'was by the irregular ftrokes, of which
there were many at that fiege, that they came to coft fo
much. Befides, the attacks of Turin in 1706, and Lifle
in 1708, were very ill conducted, and for thefe there is
no excufe.

I fhall juft obferve, that, if it is objected that fo large
a place of arms as in Fig. 17. is liable to be carried by
general affault much earlier in the fiege than the ravelin,
if a great addition is not made to the garrifon, and which
I do not believe; yet that a great faving may be made
by floping the bottom of the ditch from the falient angle
towards the face of a baftion, in fuch a manner that it
may

ground further off; for if there were no variation in the troops or ftores, that in itfelf would only oblige him to go through more fathoms meeting lefs refiftance in each fathom ; nor becaufe of the time and expence he muft beftow on making a practicable breach in the ravelin ; but becaufe of its ufe when the enemy comes near, and the ufe of the collateral ravelins.

V.

In fome places we find fimple fronts, as in Fig. 19. For the flanks and curtain I propofe a redan, as in Fig. 20. The developement of the two figures is the fame. To the ravelind method, Fig. 21. I prefer

Fig.

•

may be well feen into, and that to fuch a ditch the objection will not be made.

As to the flanks of the redoubts, there is little ufe in thofe of the front attacked ; the ufe is in thofe of the collateral fronts ; at building the place, therefore, they ought not to be raifed fo high as the creft of the glacis.

Fig. 22. Fig. 23. is given as a fimilar improvement on Fig. 5.

VI.

If there was drawn within Fig. 6. (for
inftance) parallel to it and at the proper diftance, and fo high as to fire over it, a line
of works without a ditch, fuch a place, on
the fame total of expence, would make a
better defence than Fig. 5.

On this ground I propofe, Fig. 24. 25.
to be compared with Fig. 5. Though
thefe plans were held good, it is not to be
expected that engineers would agree foon
on the height the inner line fhould be raifed to. On the one hand is to be alledged
the greater quantity of fire which may be
employed, at a greater height too, the line
which holds it almoft entirely covered from
the enemy, and in a direction different
from any other, with the equal eafe of fal-
lying

lying for a trifle more expence in the if-
fues. On the other, befides confiderations
already often employed, there may be much
ftrefs laid on the effect of fallies, particularly when joined to vigorous mining, on
which fubject the authority of Saxe, given
in a very inftructive project of fortification,
may be added, and the advantages of blow-
ing judicioufly pieces of the outer wall
may be mentioned.

VII.

In chap. 5. Siege of Rivol, Le Febvre
directs that the befieged fhould begin to fire
as foon as they know where the enemy is,
' *Le feu* (fays he) *d'une place affiegé n'eft*
' *jamais fi fort qu'au commencement du fiege ;*
' *et cela doit etre ainfi ; pour eloigner l'af-*
' *fizeant le plus qu'il eft poffible, et lui dif-*
' *puter le terrein pied à pied* *.' In that fiege

X   I

---

* He goes on here, *Lorfque l'artillerie du dehors a*

I cannot help thinking, that the garrison ought not to fire a shot till the besieger sets about his third parallel at soonest, that is, in the attack of the left, for instance. Le Febvre informs us in the same chapter, that in all the sieges of the last war, (the war 1741, in the Low Countries,) the besieged, the night of opening the trenches, either did not fire at all, or not till after midnight, and says I am *tres persuadé* that the governors had all flattered themselves that they would not be surprised. In chap. 4. § 1. he tells us, that, in the last sieges of the French in Flanders, they lost fewer men the night of opening the first parallel

than

gagné la superiorité sur celle du dedans, il n'est guere possible qui celle-ci lui resiste, et si l'assiegé ne profite pas du tems et de ses avantages des le commencement, en voulant peut etre trop economiser a quoi lui suivront ensuite ses poudres, et toutes ses autres munitions, lorsque ses batteries seront demontrés, et qu'il ne lui restera plus que quelques pieces ambulantes. I do not see what he meant here; for I cannot suppose him to have run into an error which Vauban and Bisset avoided.

than in moſt of the other nights. In this
very ſiege our author take it for granted,
that the beſieged do not fire till after the
enemy has been ſome hours at work, and
he ſuppoſes the ſoil neither favourable nor
otherwiſe. The advantage is that of employing the ſhot when he is a better mark,
and when his ſhot is more to be feared.
It may be objected, that, if he does not
fire his ammunition from the beginning,
it will be taken ; but that can happen only
from miſproportioning the ſtores to one
another, or to the troops, or from miſcon-
duct. It may be ſaid, that this makes it
his intereſt, or at leaſt engages him to perform the firſt parallel ; though it ſhould,
he can better afford it ; in ſieges we muſt
ſuppoſe that he can get what he wants, and
the place only what it ſet out with *.

VIII.

* I found, in the King's library at Berlin, a book I had
long ſearched for to no purpoſe, *Analyſi ed eſame ragionato
dell' arte della fortificazione e diſeſa delle piazze dell' Abbate
Carlo Borgo, Venezia* 1777, in which the author propoſes to
ſave

VIII.

In the fame attack of the left, Fig. 11. there are no batteries of cannon raifed between the breaching batteries on the creft of the glacis and the third parallel ; and thefe laft are covered by the crowning of the glacis. Now, I think it were much more frugal to raife between thefe. I would raife them for two ends.

Firft, To have my cannon where I had a better mark.

Secondly, To avoid covering them by my works on the glacis.

Le

fave the fire alfo, and defends fuch conduct at great length. I, however, left my fection as it ftood, becaufe I got thereby an opportunity of defending further the changes I propofe in the conftruction of places.

Le Febvre fays, chap. 16. that whatever is done by the ricochet batteries on the flanks of the attack, (they are in the first parallel) by a constant fire of the mortars of the trenches, and the musquetry without ball from the nearest parts of the approaches, cannot hinder, but the interval from covering the batteries of the third parallel to opening the breaching ones, is the time of the siege in which they must lose the most men *; and in chap. 17. that the situation of the besieger is then the most critical in the whole siege. The besieger covering his cannon, if he means to hinder the garrison from having their works before he can begin to batter in breach, in almost as good condition as they were in the first day of the siege, must do it by mortars : For the batteries in ricochet can do little. Biffet fays they did little at Bergen-op-zoom. It does not appear that they did much at Schweidnitz ; and Le

Febvre,

---

* This *expreffion* is ambiguous.

Febvre, in chap. 17. fays that, in thefe circumftances, the befieger is not always fure
of being able to make ufe of them as he
would with.

Suppofe now the ammunition of Rivol
hufbanded fo as that there remains two
thirds of it (for inftance) when the enemy
has covered his batteries on the third parallel. In this cafe there is ftill more reafon for making fuch batteries as I propofe.

IX.

If againft a pentagon five attacks (*e. g.*)
are made inftead of one, it has but the
fifth part of the troops and ftores to op-
pofe each attack.

* * * * *

The progrefs of all fciences has been
much retarded by routine. Fortification
has

has alfo felt its effects. There is perhaps
lefs reafon to expect that it fhould, in a
little time, get out of its fhackles than any
fcience of fact and exiftence.

In this fcience the opportunity of experiments has always been fmall ; the number of places fortified is fmall ; few have
accefs to fee them ; fieges rarely occur ;
the experiments coming under the eyes of
few were communicated with the more re-
ferve ; a failure would draw bad confe-
quences where the ftake played for was fo
deep. This has been the chief fubject of
attention to very few. The nomination
of an engineer to build a place is a fubject
of intrigue in the Sovereign's court, and
perhaps in half a dozen courts below his.
There is a buftle to name the director of
an attack or defence, and who is to attend
him.

Tactics

Tactics are alfo a fubject of intrigue; but in them the opportunity of experiment is endlefs. Improvement in them was fuppofed to be of more confequence, than any improvement in the other; procured much higher rewards from the Sovereign, and could place a man a great deal higher in the eyes of the world too; they have not only been the chief fubject of attention to an infinitely greater number of people in each country; but if we compare the nations to whom they have been the principal fubject of attention, we fhall find engineering has had by much the leaft. They have been cultivated by numbers whofe genius is placed in the firft rank, and that for ages paft. Yet, in the hiftory of modern tactics, we fee not only all Europe, but thefe great names, perfift, till very lately, through ages, in errors which would feem to require no great effort of acutenefs to detect. It may occur that this fubject muft be confeffed fimple, that no other account can be given of the moderate degree of refpect paid to

any

any fuccefs in it, refpect in itfelf moderate,
paid but to a very fmall number, while all
the others who follow it, or have followed
it, are neglected or forgot. That it has
not, however, been left entirely to thofe
whofe profeffion particularly it is; that the
greateft generals have had more or lefs at
ftake in fieges; have interefted themfelves,
and been interefted, whether they would or
not, in their event.

In the *firft* place, in the hiftory of other
fciences, we do not find that the fimpleft
difcoveries were the firft made. In the *next*
place, thefe great men left, in the fciences
they chiefly attended to, errors, which we
would think eafily amended. In the *laft*
place, it is certain, that none of them made
any improvement in either the attack, the
defence, or the conftruction of towns:
Though they were often engaged by every
tie to ftudy them; as if the fimplicity of
the fubject had deprived them of their u-
fual reach.

Y   It

It is not denied, that till Vauban got into employment, there was much routine in engineering; the many errors made, *en passant*, in the moſt eſtimable books, and in thoſe of an inferior order, on the chief ſubject in view, not only ſhow that the ſubject is far leſs familiar than is alledged; but excite a ſuſpicion that many opinions on the moſt important queſtions are chiefly the reſult of routine. I ſhall not enter into theſe; but I ſhall give ſome deliberate opinions of men of the firſt diſtinction, on important points, which appear ſtill more to confirm the ſuſpicion.

FOLARD,

In his Commentary on Polybius, Book I. Chap. I. pag. 47. he ſays, ' *Apres la priſe* ' *du Queſnoy ils*,' (the Allies in the war of the Spaniſh ſucceſſion). ' *inveſtiſſent Lan-* ' *ducy, (ils n'avoient que a pas a faire pour* ' *penetrer la France), qui etoit une affaire* ' *de*

' *de peu de jours, avec des forces ſi formi-*
' *dables. Les gens eclairez croioient me-*
' *me cette bicoque plus bicoque qu'elle n'etoit*
' *en effet, en jaiſant abſtraction de ſes rem-*
' *parts, et de ſes ouvrages.*' The *gens e-*
clairez muſt have had an accurate plan of
the place, for it had been long in the hands
of the French, and the ſituation of their
affairs, for ſome time before the ſiege, forced them to attend to it. The *gens eclairez,*
therefore, eſtimated the ſtrength of the
place by its works, without obſerving what
difference providing it better than uſual
would make, or, at leaſt, believing it would
make no difference worth regarding. The
author no where inſinuates that he did not
himſelf fall into the miſtake with the *gens
eclairez;* his expreſſion rather inſinuates the
contrary.

LAN-

'*Apres avoir attentivement medité sur*
'*le plan de la citadelle de Lille, dans le tems*
'*que les allies s'en etoient rendus maitres*
'*de meme que de la ville, il me sembla qu'en*
'*moins de deux mois de tems, et pour la*
'*somme de douze ou quinze mille ecus, on*
'*pourroit mettre cette citadelle en tel etat,*
'*qu'il ne seroit pas possible aux assiegeans de*
'*la reprendre par la force de l'artillerie.*
'*Je me persuadai qu'on pouvoit faire la*
'*meme chose a l'egard de Bethune et de*
'*Aix. 125,000 florins de la Hollande suf-*
'*fisoient pour ces trois places;*' . . . goes on
to prove this, and explain his plan. '*Je ne*
'*doute point qu'un bon commandant, a qui la*
'*defence d'une place construite suivant les*
'*regles que j'ai pris la liberté de proposer,*
'*seroit confié, ne fut en etat d'empecher*
'*l'ennemi d'entrer dans le chemin couvert,*
'*et qu'il en rendroit bon compte, s'il avoit*
'*seul-*

' *feulement cinq ou fix bataillons dans la*
' *place, et cinquante ou foixante pieces de*
' *canon de huit ou douze livres de balle.*'

To fuch a degree has the proportion of
the total troops and ftores of the garrifon
to thofe of the befieger been neglected.

FEUQUIERES.

Vid. his Remarks on the defence of
Tournay.

SAXE, Reveries, Book II. Chap. 1.

' *It is towards the end of a fiege, when*
' *every thing comes to be difputed by inches,*
' *that vigor and refolution are moft wanted:*
' *At which time, the greater proofs you*
' *give of thefe, the more the enemy will be*
' *difcouraged; for difcords will then begin*
' *to fpread among them; forage and provi-*
                                    ' *fions*

' sions will grow scarce, and all things
' seem to concur to their destruction If,
' moreover, they perceive that your resist-
' ance is still stronger, and that it increases
' when they expected it to diminish, they
' will be at a loss how to act, and give
' themselves totally up to despair.'

They surely need not despair of exhaust-
ing his ammunition and stores; and what
are works without arms?

Vauban's First Method.

This is completely reveted, ditch twenty
toises broad, twelve feet deep; suppose the
fire of the rampart to graze the glacis
completely.

State now another plan also completely
reveted, ditch same depth, twelve toises
broad, same glacis, and the fire of the rampart to graze it, in all its breadth, as it
does

does the other. Suppofe now batteries of
the fame height above the field, and at the
fame diftance, planted againft both.

Since the heights of the ramparts are as
their diftance from the foot of the glacis,
the portion of Vauban's rampart feen over
the glacis, fubtends at the battery a greater
angle than the portion of the lower one;
the befieger can alfo batter in breach Vauban's rampart at a greater diftance: On the
other hand, Vauban's rampart fees more
into the befieger's works. Let us leave
thefe to balance one another; engineers
will, perhaps, never agree on them. Suppofe Vauban's place provided according to
Le Febvre's rule, his own, or any other, fo
it be decently furnifhed, and the other place
the very fame. Any one who would give
a general affault to the fecond, while the
works are yet entire, ought alfo to do the
fame to Vauban's, for the narrow ditch is
ftill fo broad as to hinder him the fame. The
only advantage Vauban's has, is a mere
trifle,

trifle, (it will be allowed fo) more difficulty in the afcent: And, in the other, the
works are clofer, as well as lefs expofed.
If, at any time, earlier than ufual, he means
to give the general affault, fuppofing the
ftrength in both hufbanded the fame, as
alfo the fame attack, it is eafier for him to
give it to the higher work, as he muft be
fuppofed to have made more demolition in
it than in the other, and the greater lofs of
men he may fuftain from the higher work,
we muft fuppofe him able to repair. With
regard to regular fiege, it is fufficient to obferve, that, on the one hand, Vauban's plan
has a broader ditch for the enemy to pafs,
where it is faid he may be oppofed; and,
no doubt, he may; but the advantage is
only that of oppofing him there, rather
than elfewhere, which is juft nothing; on
the other hand, the narrow ditch brings.
the works clofer, undoubtedly an advantage. Though the difference of the height
of the ramparts be but a trifle in the length
of the fcaling ladders, yet the expence of
that

that difference, carried round a reveted place, is very confiderable. The glacis and parapet of both require the fame quantity of earth; the evacuation of the greater ditch is to that of the fmaller, in a greater proportion than its rampart is to the lower. But, when a fortrefs is done where there were no houfes, there is a vaft quantity of earth which muft be carried away; when a place already built is to be fortified, the interval between the works and it, almoft every where, affords a great deal: It is, in towns, thought a faving to fink private buildings a few feet. Without the works, earth is every where to be had, and little heights are fometimes met with that would be of ufe to the befieger.

The queftion is, between earth got out of the middle of the wide ditch, and earth got elfewhere.

It is, on the whole, almoft every where much more to the engineer's purpofe, to

Z₃   make,

make, in this method, the ditch only twelve toifes.

Now, to the firft who fortified by both a ditch and bank, it appeared excellent contrivance to do two things at once.

COCHORN's *Ditch.*

Say twelve fathom broad, and eighteen feet deep; compare this with a ditch of the fame breadth, only twelve feet deep.

Any advantages the latter has over Vauban's firft method, the former has alfo, befides the additional ftrength by the depth of the ditch. Suppofe the befieger meant to give the general affault while the ditches were entire, and the ramparts entire, or nearly fo, or the works in both equally hurt; the defcent and afcent are not only more difficult in reality, but the very appearance

pearance of the deeper ditch is much more
fuited to awe the imagination; fo that if
the latter is decently provided, the former
may be held equally defenfible, with a lefs
force. But the method univerfally appro-
ved, when a place is properly provided, is,
to weaken the garrifon, and make a large
breach, before giving the affault, if it is to
be given at all. All engineers will confefs,
that, in the regular method of approach, the
difference between pafling the deep ditch
and the other, when oppofed by equal
ftrength of garrifon, is a mere trifle. Now,
though Cochorn could revet his ditch, at
the fame, or perhaps lefs expence than
Vauban could his; yet a ditch of only the
depth of Vauban's may be reveted in Cochorn's method. As to the earth, the queftion is about only hoifting it from a greater depth, and getting it from elfewhere.

The difference of expence between the
two conftructions is great; by ufing the
one, this difference is almoft entirely faved,

till

till wanted, and then is only used (except a trifle, if people aim at nicety) in the fronts attacked : A great superiority.

But Cochorn's ditch affords earth enough for the works.

Le Febvre.

Siege of Rivol, chap. 7. § 6. ' *On fait* ' *deux ou trois attaques devant une méme* ' *place, pour en impofer a l'affiegé et divifer* ' *fes forces ; quoique d'ordinaire il n'y en ait* ' *qu'une vraie, on doit cependant les traiter* ' *toutes auffi férieufement l'une que l'autre,* ' *ou du moins le paroitre, autrement l'ennemi* ' *qui s'appercevroit bientot de la feinte, laif-* ' *feroit l'une pour donner fa principale at-* ' *tention a l'autre.*' The falfe attacks are to be carried on by this direction fo brifkly, that the befieged fhall have a difficulty in

diftinguifhing

diftinguifhing which is the true*; they muft, therefore, have, during the former part of the fiege, a good number of labour-ers, with their tools, for the falfe attacks; they muft alfo be pretty well guarded, at leaft, in proportion to the other. Why not then make them real? The thing feems perfectly clear. There is not here the leaft infinuation of exhaufting the garrifon the fooner (nor any where elfe), but expreffions fo very general, as fhow that the author had no intention of communicating any thing out of the beaten path †. It is true,

---

* The author gives inftances of places taken on the attacks meant at firft to be falfe, fo that, in fome of thefe, the deception may have been well kept up; I fay only may, becaufe there are bad reports of the Orange party; and our author informs us, that the French were fome-times carelefs in reconnoitring

† I conclude, that one part of the meaning of the ex-preffion *en impofer a l' affiege*, was to miflead him that he may make (for the time) lefs refiftance to the true, and neglect fome one of the falfe, fo far as to give the befie-ger an advantage in making the true. From the facts alluded

that there muſt be ſome quantity, beyond which all the ſtrength thrown into a place would be of no uſe, and if a place were ſo provided, making more real attacks than one (or, indeed, falſe either) would be only more loſs, if not delay: But, on the ſlighteſt examination, it will be confeſſed, that no place has ever yet had that quantity, or any thing near it. As a place may alſo be ſo very weakly provided that there is little uſe in a falſe attack, or in more than one true one.

This laſt is not the queſtion here.

Le Febvre,

Siege of Rivol, chap. 5. § 2. ſays, ' *Le* ' *feu d'une place aſſiegé n'eſt jamais ſi fort* ' *qu'au*

alluded to in the preceding note, he never inſinuates any thing of the treachery of the governours; even a treacherous governour might give an advantage when he did not mean it.

' *qu'au commencement du fiege ; et cela doit*
' *'etre ainfi, pour eloigner l'affiegeant le plus*
' *qu'il eft poffible, et lui difputer le terrein pied*
' *a pied.*' As if the troops and ftores in
the place were unlimited. In this very
fiege, on the attack of the left it is certainly foon enough to begin firing when the
befieger fets about his third parallel, which
is on the fourth night of the fiege.

He-informs us himfelf, in the fame chapter, that, in all the fieges of the laft war,
(the war 1741 in the Low Countries), the
befieged, the night of opening the trenches,
either did not fire at all, or not till after
midnight, adding, I am *tres perfuadé* that
the governours had all flattered themfelves
that they would not be furprifed : Alfo, in
chap. 4. § 1. That in the laft fieges of the
French in Flanders, they loft fewer men
the night they opened the firft parallel than
in the run of the other nights. In this
very fiege, he takes it for granted, that the
befieged do not fire till after the enemy has
been

been some hours at work, and he supposes the soil neither favourable, nor otherwise.

The question is, therefore, merely the use of so many shot when the enemy is at a greater or less distance.

The expression he uses is that of a general rule, which includes sieges where mining is employed: Yet, if the place is ill provided, the conduct I propose is still less to be disputed. If a place, indeed, were provided, as no place ever was, nor Rivol in particular, such conduct (Vid. preceding instance) would be pure loss.

The question is only the shot fired in three days; it cannot, surely be pretended, in the case of Rivol, that this quantity must, if not fired then, be found in the magazine.

His reason is, not that the variation this would cause in the repair would be as hurt-
ful

ful as the wafte objected to; for, befides, that fuch variation, though, on the whole, more material, could be guarded againft in providing the place, he takes no notice of the circumftance, but gives other reafons. It is true, that, in his method, the befieger paffes through more fathoms under the fire of the place; but, in mine, after paffing fome unrefifted, he meets more refiftance in each fathom of the remainder; the facts he has given fhow, that, in his method, the additional quantity wherein I would not beftow oppofition, is paffed through with little lofs, and that furely might be believed on much lefs authority.

He goes on ' *Lorfque l'artillerie du de-* ' *hors a gagné la fuperiorité fur celle du* ' *dedans, il n'eft quere poffible que celle ci* ' *lui refifte, et fi l'affiege ne profite pas du* ' *tems, et de fes avantages des le com-* ' *mencement, a quoi lui ferviroient fes poudres* ' *et toutes des autres munitions, lorfque fes* ' *batteries feront demontées, et qu'il ne lui*

' *reftera*

'restera plus que quelques picces ambulan-
' tes.

Of the Bastion and Curtain. The Routine Line.

Where no account is kept of the improvements made, where any account taken has been kept private, or even has not got into the public, it is difficult, if not impoffible, for moft to fee how they were affected by routine. Even with a tolerable hiftory of the practice of ages, we might be mifled from omiffions in our monuments, and fufpect routine where there was none, as well as novelty. Even with hiftories a degree more complete, there is ftill room for hefitation.

The hiftory of the invention of the baftion given by Deidier in his *Parfait Inge-nieur*

nieur François, is fo natural, that, allow-
ing for fome deviations, which neither
could nor ought be noticed in fo general a
view, we cannot believe it very different
from what really happened. After the
middle of the fifteenth century, we find
fuch works on foot, that the trains of artillery then brought to fieges, were able
(for aught we know, in fpite of all attempts
to repair) to make a practicable breach in
a day or two, and that from the firft ground
the batteries were made on. While building and repairing were fo ill underftood
making the flank of the baftion *fichant*,
might juftly be efteemed a very good contrivance. This pofition, however continued it is well known to be directed by a
long lift of authors, long after the neceffity
was removed. Errard of Bar, engineer to
Henry the Great of France, made his
flank perpendicular to the face, keeping it
fafe; after him we find a long lift who,
for the fame reafon, made the flank perpendicular to the curtain. At length, however,

ever, a better pofition has been of late a-
greed on. But the flank fichant continued
not only long after the firft neceffity, but
after the efcalade itfelf was fcarce ever
feen ; becaufe it was not thought of till
the breach was good, the garrifon of a vigorous governor was by this time exhauft-
ed, or before, and no other would dream
of rifking it. The long flank, however,
continued ftill in favour, though no one
could fhow that the half of it, or little
more, was not enough. Biflet propofed
to fhorten the perpendicular fo as to make
the flank of fixteen fathoms, befides the
flanks of the gorges. This change had
many advantages ; in particular, when joined to the flank of the face given in his fecond method, one fhould have fuppofed no
oppofition would have been made to it.
Yet, from what we find in the books printed fince thefe improvements were fuggeft-
ed, and from the work of that excellent
engineer never having got to a fecond edi-
tion, we fee that they are neglected. The
baftion,

baftion, though originally contrived againft
the efcalade and the paffage of the ditch,
continues ftill the element of regular fortification, though the efcalade has been out
of the queftion for a century paft, although,
for fo long a time, not only the paffage of
the ditch, but every part of a fiege, has
changed its face; and though a bare in-
fpection fhows, that a redan, in all common cafes, might be fubftituted to its flanks
and curtain to great advantage.

Of Wet Ditches.

The confideration of thefe gives, perhaps, the chief objection againft the reafonings laid down above. It may be faid,
that the dimenfions of thefe are lefs than
thofe of dry ditches; that thefe guard better againft the general affault than dry
ditches; that engineers, therefore, were in
the conftruction of ditches plainly guided
by the facility of the general affault, and
thought

thought fuch dimenfions as **Fig. 3.** too
fmall.

In the firft place, I am yet to learn that
the dimenfions of ditches have been much
or often altered on account of the water
in them, except in preferring a broad fhal-
low ditch to a narrow deep one, or that
the general opinion of engineers is, that
that there ought to be much other alteration on that account. In Le Febvre's Rivol, the great ditch is twelve feet deep,
and twenty toifes broad, the fize attributed
to Vauban's dry ditches, and admitted to
be fufficient without the fix feet of water;
the ditch of the ravelin the fame depth, and
fourteen toifes broad, agreed to be enough,
though dry.

It is obvious, that the water renders the
paffage of the ditch more difficult, either
in affault or in regular fiege; and, therefore, it is no wonder if an engineer, free-
ing himfelf a little from routine, fhould
content

content himfelf with dimenfions fomewhat
lefs. But even this may have coft time,
may have begun, or been fometimes ufed
from being confined in the fum allotted
for building the places, or even from fraud
or difputes about ground. And I think
it may be plainly fhown, that the opinions
ftated in the objection were not thofe of
the engineers who did make the deviation.
Compare the plan of Rivol (e. g.) with another whofe ditches are of the fame depth,
the great ditch only fourteen toifes broad,
and that of the ravelin ten. The garrifon
that provides Rivol tolerably well, will not
be pretended a bad provifion for the other.
Narrowing the ditch gives many advantages ; the works are lower, therefore lefs
expenfive, and feen at a lefs angle from
the field ; they are clofer, and the befieger,
it is agreed, has much lefs ground to erect
batteries againft the flanks. This laft advantage is much infifted on by all engineers in treating of the falient angle of the

baition

baſtion and Cochorn's ditch *. All theſe,
it will be allowed, overbalance the advantage of the height of Rivol. Where much
of the water of the ditch is gained from
within itſelf, there cannot be a worſe place
to get earth from than the ditch. Nothing,
therefore, but routine could have hindered
the ditch from being narrowed.

Where the ground eaſily permits mining,
and the ditch is wet, there is leſs reaſon
againſt the alterations I propoſe.

Of Irregular Fortification.

Though I thought that the methods I
oppoſe could be defended againſt all I have
ſaid

---

* It is ſufficient for my argument that this is ſuppoſed no inconſiderable advantage. In reality it is a trifle.
If he extends his battery on the glacis it coſts him ſome-
what more labour. As far as he extends them on the
co.. rſcarp he conſtructs them at more labour; but big
merlons are ſtronger.]

faid, I fhould think that the great variety
of plans that has been propofed, is not
more ufeful by giving different fcales of
expence, than by giving different pofitions
of works.

On confidering the different expedients
by which the difadvantages of fituation are
corrected or eluded, it will be allowed,
that, if I have fucceeded in fhowing that a
fingle line is fufficient in even ground, it
may often be found the propereft in unc-
ven ground. Where its faces were fo fhort
as not to contain fire enough, I would, in
general, prefer cavaliers * to outworks, as
alfo where, on other accounts, I built two
lines. If my opinions on hufbanding the
ammunition and troops of the place are

B b juft,

---

* I do not mean to limit the ufe of cavaliers to un-
even ground ; I think that, in my own plans of regular
fortification, fome little things of the kind would here
and there be worth the expence. To them they are of
more value than to the ufual methods.

juft, the engineer is more at liberty in choofing his plan. I need not enter into cafes extremely bad.

* * * * *

If cremailleres (invented by Fallois) are ufed inftead of the glacis and covered way, (I think them preferable) there will be the lefs to objeᴄt to the alterations I propofe.

* * * * *

Though it fhould be held that, in the cafes confidered, I may in fome inftances have propofed laying out too little money on the works, yet I flatter myfelf it will be allowed, that, in the plans now preferred, the expence of them is too great by far.

Explanation

All except No. 11. 12. 13. 14. 15. are done from a fcale half an inch to twenty-five fathoms or toifes, fold in the common cafes.

In all, the fire from the rampart is fuppofed to graze the glacis equally.

Fig. 1. 2. and 5. are ftated only demi-reveted, and of courfe thofe compared with them, if they were ftated fully reveted, the objeĉtions to them would have ftill more force : But that feems abandoned of late.

I fuppofe the places of arms and the covered way occupied very much by cannon, and either on high carriages or in fomething like the way direĉted in Saxe's Reveries ;

Reveries; a few of thefe will do more than all the troops it can contain ; but they muft be attended by guards, befides thofe who work them. I have drawn no traverfes in the covered way, becaufe, though thefe muft be had when the enemy is at fome diftance, yet, when he comes fo near as that there is fome chance of his fucceeding in an affault on it, the beft defence is, to caft down or carry away the traverfes, and withdraw all the people who are above ground.

Fig.

Fig. 1. Great ditch	14 fathom broad	14 feet deep.
Ditch of the ravelin	10	10
Fig. 3. Great ditch	8	9
Ditch of the ravelin	6	7
Fig 2. Great ditch	10	18
Ditch of the ravelin	6	14
Ditch of the lunette	3	10
Fig. 4. Great ditch	6	14
Ditch of the ravelin	6	14
———— lunette	3	10
Fig. 5. Great ditch	14	14
Ditch of ravelin	10	10
——- counterguard	7	7
Fig. 6. Ditch	7	10
Fig. 7. Ditch	8	9
Fig. 8.	6	12

O F